The Schaefer Diaries

I0746238

A NOVEL OF ALTERNATE HISTORY

Daniel H Lessin

Black Labrador Creations LLC

*This book is dedicated to adventurers of a kind,
with an open heart and an open mind.*

A Note to Readers

This book comes with some caveats. *The Schaefer Diaries* is a work of alternate history. The First World War did not happen in this fashion. Some of the personalities, locales, and battles are fictional, whilst elements of others are fabricated for lack of information available. The strong language and, at times, morally questionable viewpoints taken in this book, meant to be historically correct, do not represent the author's views.

As the author personally feels that both factions blundered horribly in the First World War, he does not mean to suggest, even as the story is focused on them, that the Germans had the just side of World War One. There were many people of courage and honor on both sides. There were many scoundrels, fools, and incompetents on both sides as well.

Diarist's Note, 5 March 1933

As I compile my cautionary writings in the blessed sanctuary of Costa Rica—a sun-kissed locale where I can truly be at peace amidst the tittering quetzals and toucans of the cloud forests, or perhaps watch the tortoises plod along the fine-grained, sandy beaches (where I might practice my breaststroke in the clear waters and grow peppers in my garden whilst chasing Moritz, my pet German Shepherd)—I would like to begin by introducing myself.

My name is Maxwell Schaefer.

As I should not like to be defined by what I do for a living, I shall say I am a human being who has, at times in his life, enjoyed much revelry and good fortune. In such moments, I had the wealth to engage in whatever hobbies I did enjoy. Foremost amongst them, for a time, was aviation. This would lead to my meteoric rise and eventual fall from grace.

I was born in Vienna in the year 1894. My early years are cloudy, but I have been told I grew up amongst the Jewish educated class. My father was a university professor, making enough money by himself for Mother to tend to him and me closely. At this time, Vienna was a land of intellectualism and cultural diversity. The Austro-Hungarian Empire was a place for my people and many others to enjoy relative tolerance and freedom to pursue our dreams. Our people were valued as businessmen and bankers, amongst other specified professions.

Until Lueger came.

By God, I hope never to see his ilk in power again.

In 1897, Karl Lueger at last became mayor of Vienna by demand of the Pope. Lueger had been elected to power numerous times but had been declined authority by our protector, Emperor Franz Josef. By Mayor Lueger's order, a horrific rash of anti-Semitism ensued, with acts of unspeakable violence being committed against my people by his "Christian Social Party," which was populated by the ignorant and easily manipulated; the party pledged to serve "the little people." It was a terrifying time—we were purged from the university and from politics, with our very rights as citizens questioned. Rather than fight such cruelty and corruption, my family and I fled to Germany, where we were welcomed by the government, if perhaps not all the citizenry, of the Fatherland. However dishonorable and tragic the act—to flee rather than to fight—it also took great courage to admit we no longer belonged to or believed in Austria-Hungary.

Or so my parents said.

I was so young, I could not remember it much beyond the citizenry yelling at us and throwing potatoes, tomatoes, and other such foods as we stacked our suitcases into the boots of motor cars or onto trains bound for the lands beyond. But it brought such pain to my parents to mention this horrific past, to hear them talk about the wrongdoings they sustained, that I could only surmise the trauma our people had suffered. This engendered a mistrust of all things Austro-Hungarian in me at a young age. Meanwhile, the hopeful way my parents spoke of Germany, it had gained my dreams and youthful, idealistic trust.

It was painful to leave our home, but with the help of some wealthy relatives, we made our escape to East Prussia. It was there that I recall most of my early memories. I spent much time playing ball in the well-maintained and civilized, but still pretty and, to an adventurous child such as myself, mysterious, Königsberg countryside with my new friends whilst my family built a prosperous cheese business. For you must understand, dear Diary, that not all professors are pure academics, and many—like my father—were hands-on and savvy, learning from the mistakes of businessmen in literature and in economics texts.

Two particularly wonderful friends who come to mind, despite their not being of the faith, were my playmates Ludwig and his sister, Christianne. The first time we met, I was cautiously exploring my new home with my family. As we walked by a rather striking Tudor mansion, the door opened and, ignoring the chastisement coming from inside the mansion, two little imps, around my size, though blonde-haired, blue-eyed, and admittedly better built and fed, giggled and gamboled their way down the steps of their house. Deliberately defying their parents' instructions to not engage with the new Jewish family in town, these two children offered their hands in friendship and patted me on the back, making their first of many sorties to introduce me to Königsberg and play with me, oftentimes bearing sausage and cheese, the latter humorously bought from my own father's business. Of course, I could not eat the former, but was very pleasant about the whole affair. How could I not be? Ludwig spoke passionately about his love of animals, especially horses, and a desire to open a riding stable to teach young equestrians. "You can be one too, if you wish!" he said, smiling happily, when I expressed appreciation for his goals.

Christianne, meanwhile, blushingly expressed a hope that she might travel the world with whatever husband she might find, as though it were unlikely. Ludwig was quick to support his sister, promising her "the best husband one could find, be he English or Turkish or even Jewish!" Us being starry-eyed youths, we paid little mind to cultural differences and simply enjoyed each other's company.

It should have always been so.

As the years marched on, Ludwig gained, in addition to his youthful affinity for horses, a love of automobiles, whilst cutting a most handsome figure when on foot with his ramrod-straight posture, hands clasped behind his back whilst whistling merry tunes in his hunter-green jacket. A veritable Apollo he was, be it with his grasp of music (though he never seemed to take much interest in it) or his hunting acumen. And how he could ride! He would mount and become one with his chestnut thoroughbred, riding like the wind, but always sure to wear his beaked black helmet on horseback, his eyes dancing with a refined-but-endearing sort of joyous lunacy that drove me into the depths of longing. Though he had no such protection when he attired himself in his scarf and goggles whilst riding his motor car, he looked equally dashing—aristocratic and suave with his charismatic command over his somewhat newfangled machinery.

I, not wishing to lose his interest for fear of losing my friend, casually followed suit. I have many not-so-fond memories of attempting to vault myself atop a mount, only to have it begin to move as I did so, for though I have much love and respect for nature, I have little compatibility with it, and no time to practice the equestrian arts, as my father wished that I focus more on my studies. I split my time and barely satisfied both parties with little time for my own interests—swimming, gardening, and dog rearing. These interests I silently cultivated more in theory than in practice, though I certainly read up extensively on them. Through my adventures in reading, I concluded that I'd very much love to swim in the crystal-clear waters of the Caribbean realms, discovering exotic deep-sea creatures. Also, in my fascination with canines, I began to recognize even the most unusual dog breeds with ease and noticed the prolific number of uses for a German Shepherd, hoping to get one of my own someday, perhaps to guard crops I could cultivate.

For all my academic hard work, cultivating my own interests, following those of my friends with a feigned fascination, and planning for my future, it was Ludwig's sister, Christianne, who was the practical one. Hoping to make a good accounting of herself as a diligent woman of the era, she worked hard to perform odd jobs around the neighborhood befitting her sex, accruing a small personal wage. She was comely, with long blonde hair, elegantly plaited, as well as full hips and soft white hands, but for all her kindnesses, neither she, nor any other women, appealed to me romantically.

Not in the way Ludwig did, at least.

I knew it was different, but it always felt so special to hear his voice calling out my name, the attention he paid to me with his steely gaze and his advice in horsemanship: I learned both this art and the art of the motor car from him and was not only thankful—I was in awe of his abilities and romanticized him as a great polymath!

For indeed, between the three of us, our interests were diverse, but we did our best to remain close friends and to dabble in each other's fascinations.

Or at least, I did theirs.

This endured with some success, but for some time I was never really looked upon with any great appreciation by Ludwig and Christianne's father, Mr. Becker, a big angry lug of a ruddy-faced fellow with an enormous nose and an angry eye (the other one was made of glass—he was a wounded veteran of the Franco-Prussian War and highly xenophobic) who, upon realizing he couldn't banish me from his family's life altogether (his children being mischievous and going behind his back when needed to experience the "Jewboy"), he instead barely acknowledged me and, when forced to, looked upon me with a cold indifference.

This abruptly changed to a moderated extent one day when the four of us went out boating along the Danube River. As we maneuvered amongst the many pleasure boats dotting the river, the waves gently lapping against our craft whilst the sun beats down upon us and our friends, the terns and pelicans, one enormous vessel belonging to the children's father's business rival, struck our vessel on a wide, swinging arc. Mister Becker, observing our progress near the bow of the ship, fell overboard. Impulsively jumping in after him and putting my secretly cultivated swimming skills to the test, I risked my life to bring him ashore, the frigid water lapping against us both as I exerted great force to slowly, exhaustingly, drag him to safety, where we both lay on the Danube's banks, shivering. Recognizing my bravery with a curt nod, Mister Becker collapsed, his prosthetic eye falling out of its socket as he was carried away by his sailors, leaving me to be assisted by Ludwig and Christianne.

After that dramatic incident, Mister Becker proceeded to tend to me and my family's needs in his own way as they arose, providing business opportunities and money in subtle ways, attempting to be anonymous. It was almost as though he hoped never to be connected to us and certainly never acknowledged it, being the cold reserved person he just happened to be. Modest also? Perhaps. A man of honor, certainly, despite his bigotry.

If there is honor in bigotry.

The most important day in which Mister Becker played a colossal role, however, was the day in which I joined the Imperial German Air Force, and it is with that that I will begin my modest compilation of excerpts from my personal wartime diaries.

3 November 1913

So begins the official diaries of me, that is I, Maxwell Schaefer, a young gentleman of nineteen tender years who has decided to make a profession of his hobby. I cut my long, curly locks and took some amount of time to strengthen and hone my porky, flabby physique through much exercise and some starvation—things I loathe with the greatest intensity. I managed to enact them through willpower and the practice of my butterfly, an exhausting stroke I practiced while on holiday with the Beckers yet again along the Danube. I am at last able to pursue for a living the calling I have eaten, breathed, and dreamed of since a year ago to this day—FLIGHT!

It all started whilst joyriding across Königsberg with some fellow bon vivants, ladies and gentlemen alike, all wildly attractive and well monied, save for myself, and all crowded into my bosom friend Ludwig's latest automobile, with me taking up more room than I felt comfortable doing, as usual. Wind in our hair and lager in hand, we were laughing and having a fine time, until a strange contraption of wire and wood bore down upon us from over the rounded, rolling hills beyond, flying low and nearly clipping our vehicle as we gasped and pointed at its approach.

We knew this to be an aeroplane, of course, but they are a rare sight in these days and to see one up close was an unusual delight. Ludwig, surprised by its sudden arrival, let out a great shout and spun his steering wheel in an attempt to avoid it. This was an unnecessary gesture, as the aeroplane was not about to hit us, but my beloved friend was nonetheless rewarded for his efforts as we collided with the avenue of trees spanning the roadside. Though our machine was totaled, only Ludwig's pride was seriously injured. I only received a slight bump on the head. This was easily ignored in the excitement of the matter at hand, and most of us looked back on the event with a great deal of amusement.

I had fallen in lust—quite suddenly, and likely at first, in my boredom—with aviation. It was my destiny, Ludwig and I decided, to take to the skies. After inundating the filthy but willowy, elegantly mustachioed, and extremely apologetic operator who had then landed nearby, with questions as to the workings of his craft and of his own origins, I told him of my suddenly aroused but great interest in the art of aviation and asked where I could learn to fly. With a little push from the gentleman—a striking young experimental pilot from France named Henri DuCoq who had just come from a tour in Costa Rica and had been flying a new test model here in Germany—it was not much later that I aspired to gain entry to the Frankfurt Aviation Society, composed of a few men of wealth whose dreams, like my own, had wings. During these exciting times, Henri and I kept in close correspondence, he regaling me with his various exciting travels and aeronautic deeds of daring do, and I keeping him posted on my training. Over time, however, I realized that my letters had begun to sound needy and embittered. What's more, it slowly became apparent to me that there might be more to his dispatches than met the eye. I find myself concerned as to the intentions of my beloved mentor, Monsieur DuCoq. He is assuredly a lovely fellow, and a gentleman (for aren't all pilots so?), but the way he writes . . . Diary, does he have ulterior motives regarding his interest in me? He makes references to his recollection of my "handsome ursine physique," remarks on many sights he's seen that remind him of me and concludes his letters with the valedictory "with much love and affection."

I wonder if he might be attracted to me.

In a romantic sense.

Stranger still, not only am I flattered, but I am undecided as to how I feel about him in response and may have taken an interest in him in return. He is a truly remarkable fellow, but I daresay the world will not take kindly to this kind of attraction.

I had best, for both our sakes, burn these dispatches and ignore future ones. It pains my heart to do so, but even as I appreciate his mentorship and acknowledge that there may be a spark of interest—indeed, far more than I expected in a mentor, our respective safeties come first.

Yes.

It is best I try to forget about him.

Though at times I wish I needn't and had not burned the letters. For though the Society recognized me as a fellow aviator, I was nonetheless singled out for my faith and non-German heritage, causing me to be lonely.

True, I had the rights and responsibilities of a club member after I entered the organization with the assistance of my friend the pilot and the influence of Mr. Becker. He had heard of my interests from Ludwig and was convinced to assist me—some strategically placed blocks of Feta and Havarti, lovingly borrowed from my family's stock, helped. I was given as much tutelage as the next trainee pilot, yet I feel as though I never received truly equal recognition. Despite my natural talents and skills, it was some time before I was trusted behind the aerocraft controls, forced to fly a desk instead for weeks before. I breezed through written exams with ease, but no passion; what's more, I was politely snubbed in the ornate clubhouse decorated with photographs of past graduating classes and, curiously enough, show dogs and championship football squads. It was here where we aspiring pilots so often met for whiskey, cheese, and crackers, as well as poker and bocce.

With my loneliness consuming me from within whilst I was not in flight, I frequently leaned on my good friend from home, Ludwig, who himself had joined the military and was in a reserve cavalry battalion. How dashing he looked in uniform! With his well-turned ankle and perfect proportions and toned muscle! He was so handsome and brave, both qualities that sparked long-held feelings similar to striking flint against steel. I must be more attentive to my admiration going forwards, as I fear the resulting conflagration would burn our friendship to the ground. I had always thought him naturally charismatic, of course, and envied him the ease with which he fit naturally into his regiment. He thrived amongst his fellows, engaging heavily in polo, steeplechases, and dressage, as well as fencing and wrestling. As such, his responses were few and far between, but even in between tales of his great exploits, he managed to spare some pity for his old friend's sake, down on my luck as I was. He was a great comfort and, in honesty, tales of his success were just as morale raising as his attempts to cheer me up. I was glad to have a confidant.

Finally, after six plodding months, the courtesy of being disregarded and my development as a pilot stunted, I achieved several solo flights to my name and began to catch up to my peers. This started when my instructor, old Richard Mueller, who, tired of my constant nattering, finally changed his mind regarding the subtle but deliberate slowing of my studies after witnessing enduring proof that I was not only diligent in my studies but that I would not allow myself to be shunted in the face of my fellow students. My bribe of some excellent Muenster probably helped too. That fateful day I was called upon to inspect the craft assigned to me for blemishes and abrasions and, upon finding none, I cautiously climbed into the aeroplane, a homely old Bleriot clunker, my hands shaking and my heart pounding. This is what I had waited months on end for! With the supervision of Mister Mueller—a tiny, elderly, but surprisingly spry, thickly mustachioed individual with a beard like a goat, who, for all my efforts to gain his eye and fit in, still could not remember my name and irritatingly referred to me as "Jew"—I turned on the engine as the mechanics spun the propeller, and away we went!

Now, I had heard propellers from other craft as my compatriots would take off and enjoy their flights whilst I jealously watched them from my paperwork, a burning sensation in my chest, but I never expected the one I sat in front of to be so loud! I nearly lost control as I jolted in my seat, before regaining my composure and baltering down the runway, speechless in my words, my thoughts scattered to the winds.

I was free!

Though I was sure better planes would supplant this one for speed and maneuverability, in the moment, having experienced nothing like this before, it handled like a dream! *Indeed, it could do anything*, I thought, as I wafted about the enthralling blue canvas, mine to paint, warping the wings back and forth to turn. I climbed! I dove (if gently)! So excited was I to be in the cockpit at last that Mueller, serving as my copilot, had to remind me more than once to be gentle with the controls. How could I, though, having waited for this moment for so long?! I couldn't even control my stupid grin as Mueller gently took over and affected a bumpy but successful landing as my compatriots gathered below to congratulate "The Flying Jew" on his first jaunt amidst the clouds.

For all the anti-Semitic indignities I had received—which, let us face facts, I had grown used to (at least the country protects our right to practice our faith and to exist!)—this experience and future ones like it compensated for them. I had become obsessed with my new art and learned much from the company I kept, as I was determined to rise above their snobberies and prove I was better than them. Looking back, I concluded that I possessed a kindly, genteel personality, there for any man jack of them at the drop of the hat, but that my social status (theirs being barons and counts, mine being the son of an Austrian academic turned *merchant*) and religious background (Jewish, of course) were, to their mind, dubious. It stung me greatly. I was never invited to holiday parties, told I would not understand the importance of Christ's birth, nor of his resurrection. Indeed, they frequently mistook me, in my well-kept but simple habit, for a trainee mechanic, tasked with tending to their aerocraft. Stuck in a quandary between wishing to stay true to my roots, but also wishing to be looked upon as an upstanding person by these barons and professors, I, dearly desiring their esteem, took drastic action, joining the Fliegertruppen—The Imperial German Air Service.

Now, please understand that I am a man who prefers peace and always will, but in serving the Fatherland, I shall be able to fly and maintain aerocraft to my heart's content, gain the respect of my fellow German countrymen, retain my Jewish beliefs with less judgement—as I will be serving Kaiser and Fatherland above all—and be paid as well. Were I to go to war, I would at worst help observe enemy positions for the ground forces below from the safety of the skies, but even that is a tremendously unlikely possibility. Surely I'd never have to kill anyone. This is 1913! A golden age of peace and prosperity!

My parents were beside themselves upon being told as much. Wealthy and protective of their own kind, they felt themselves above military service for any nation, and subscribed to the newfangled Zionism of Mister Hertzl so popularly entrenched in the minds of the people of letters in my faith. Their beliefs—that their nation was that of Israel, not the nation that welcomed, housed, and fed them, allowing us to rise from destitution, build our own livelihoods, and grow rich and prosperous—galled me. It was no wonder people continued to look upon us with concern, even now. As we gave back to the community with our exotic cheeses, I, contrary to my parents' angry claims, felt that we of the faith must also contribute our finest to the defense of our friends and family within *this* nation, as well as that of our allies, that we may earn a place here. Did not the goyim do the same?

At least Ludwig was delighted for me, whooping gaily and clapping me on the back. "You will show them yet, Maxwell Schaefer!" He cried. "You're doing the Lord's own work, for he is a man of war, and now? So are you!"

Ignoring my parents' outrage, I found myself deployed to FFA 10, based, for now, like my family, out of East Prussia, one of the few but rapidly growing squadrons in the air arm of the German military.

I had spent too much time basking in the indulgences of the upper-middle class. It was a good life, but if I was to progress as a human, I would need to endure discomfort.

It was time to make a man of myself.

Having just made my appearance at our aerodrome—a rather bustling but disciplined, very straitlaced, well-protected hub complete with a garrison of soldiers, as well as perfect lines demarking the runways and ugly, low-ceilinged, but well-protected wooden plane hangars and barracks based out of the East Prussian countryside—I made the acquaintance of Rittmeister Erwin Schilling, a stern man with a bald head as well as a gold-rimmed monocle covering his right eye. These features glared down from above his walrus-like mustachio—a third distinguishing trait. He had a slight stutter and seemed to want to make up for the impediment with the instilling of harsh discipline on others. His penetrating eyes engendered great fear as they glared into the very depths of my soul. It was almost at once that I began to think I had made a mistake of joining the force, but I nonetheless offered my hand in friendship, the better to make the best of a bad situation. Schilling proceeded to grab my arm and forced it into a salute, explaining, "This is your greeting now. Go meet the others," and dismissed me. It was an embarrassing exchange, but in hindsight I should have expected no less from a military man. I immediately made it my goal to impress him with my skill and courage in future interactions.

The life of an airman is far more brutal than I first thought, however, and as I looked about the aerodrome and watched men practicing martial arts, men drilling and being shouted at, and men being punished publicly, I caught myself grimacing. Perhaps the enlisted ranks are not the place for a man of delicate, academic grooming. But if I was to prove myself, I would have to acclimate and become another cog in the war machine. Only then I began to truly realize that, whilst this squadron is a club of like-minded men, it is a far cry from the delightfully intellectual, if snobbish, club of eccentrics I once enjoyed. At least they appeared to be a less discriminatory group when it came to my faith.

At least, to my face.

At least, initially.

As I remarked before, 1913 has been a year of relative stability and I imagine 1914 to be much of the same. Even though Britain appears to be none too pleased with our ever-growing industry (and navy!), I am nearly positive that our two leaders, related by blood, would never come to blows with one another. Though nations have postured and alliances have been forged, it is exactly those alliances—both the Triple Entente of France, Russia, and Italy (with Italy having broken from our alliance, fresh from their victory over the Turks in 1912 and eyeing Austro-Hungarian holdings greedily), as well as our own Quadruple Alliance (a sort of "Central Powers" of Germany, the aforementioned Austria-Hungary, and the Ottoman Empire, as well as Bulgaria) that assuredly will deter our nations and possibly those of others from going to war with one another. Even as they strut about and field great armies to impress one another. I am quite confident any talk of actual war will lead to a stalemate and no full-blown conflict. This inaction will all conclude in a great loss of capital for all involved, but fortunately no loss of lives. I, for one, am just pleased I shall be able to fly machines and be amongst the birds! I care little for the prospect of conflict about which some pessimists and war hawks murmur, and hope it does not happen.

For all my bluster, dear Diary, it must be admitted that I do worry about France. Not possessed of a peaceably inclined relationship with our most eccentric leader, Kaiser Wilhelm II, and likely spoiling for revenge after our successful liberation of Alsace and Lorraine some forty years ago, their republic has recovered well and nurses a fearsome hatred of our country, and their recent anti-Semitism in the form of their treatment of Capitaine Alfred Dreyfus shows their true face toward the Jewish population of the world. This outrages me further, pushing me even more into the arms of Germany, whose government shows more indifference than cruelty toward their Jewish population, even if individual citizens may feel otherwise. However, should France, in some outrageous reality, rally their allies to arms against us, we would be hard-pressed to face a simultaneous assault from both the East and West, especially with our less-than-inspired roster of allies.

And so, I leave you, dear Diary, a slightly disappointed new addition to FFA 10 with a guardedly optimistic view of the future! Though I do not expect it at first, I am sure my parents will soon overcome their current feelings of outrage and instead marvel at all the good I am doing for myself, the family name, and the nation. They are sure to write me many letters, as will Ludwig, my companion in blood, whose cavalry unit has been deployed (aviators of the ground as they are), and his sister, Christianne. I know this for certain because she, upon hearing of my interest in enlisting, kissed me goodbye, promising to be true to me. I had not the cruelty, or perhaps not the heart, to tell her I do not favor her that way and would instead prefer to while the next few years away with my band of brothers. She was fine company, however, and would be more than welcome to come along in addition, perhaps as a nurse. In fact, anyone of sound heart would be welcome to come along on our adventures!

Now, to begin my military training!

4 March 1914

Diary,

As perfidious Albion seeks to maintain their crushing monopoly on trade and naval tonnage at sea, we of Germany defiantly ignore the threats of both their forces and our opposites in the Triple Entente, our shipbuilding programmes forging ever ahead. Meanwhile, we fly the occasional training patrol in our friendly skies above Königsberg, concerning ourselves only slightly with the Russian Bear's developments in the east. Whilst I am confident they would never commit an act of war against us, they belong to that damnable enemy alliance and command great fortunes, military might, and a strong, ever-evolving railroad network. These are definite reasons to keep a close eye on them.

Meanwhile, I find myself acclimating to a military life at last.

I woke up this morning to a kit inspection as usual. Today, however, I forgot to put away my Shabbos candleholders and an extensive room search ensued as various articles of my faith were looked upon with suspicion. "What the blazes do you need this candleholder for, *Flieger* Schaefer?" Feldwebel Evan Albrecht inquired of me, as though to grind me down into conformation with his interpretation of military code, even though we were permitted to retain such pieces. Much as I wanted to knock some sense into him, I had been bred to defuse conflicts with words and learned how to speak the language of the military man and respond quickly and with much deference to my superiors. "Religious articles, sir!" I roared. "I hope to keep the faith whilst serving Kaiser and Fatherland!"

My initial response to his aggressive inquisition would be to tear up, or at least call it to the attention of the squadron leader, but to face facts, I was the new addition to the squadron and needed to set a good precedent. Thus, I convinced myself that perhaps this form of hazing was meant less out of malice and instead meant to make a less impulsive, less temperamental man of me.

Fortunately, this was not needed of me . . . yet.

Though I expected a neutral response—as if in clockwork tandem to my rebuttal, perhaps an "Oh, that's right. You're a Jew. See that it doesn't become an issue," or some such—much to my surprise, he expressed great enthusiasm!

"Teach me," he replied, a smile crossing his features as we crowded in close, admiring the craftsmanship behind the pieces, and later we did place candles in the holders and set them alight as I murmured the blessings over them. The man proved to be a perfectly well-intentioned fellow after all. Just trying to follow his orders, was all.

Brimming with excitement, I promised to treat him to some challah bread later.

Despite this social success, do not misunderstand me when I say the Imperial German Air Corps very much put that side of me to the test, with strict discipline in etiquette as well as with respect to the physique. Running, not to mention push-ups, sit-ups, jumping jacks, and squats abounded as we capered amongst the exercise grounds, learning drill maneuvers and attending flight seminars. Later, to eat in our serviceable, if rather spartan and sparsely crewed mess, I often selected oatmeal and raisins and eggs, served in the pilot's mess. A reasonable fare, if not particularly tasty and definitely lacking in my ingredient of choice (a serious tragedy—eggs go so well with a sharp cheddar). I did have a brief argument with the cook, however, who insisted I try his sausages too, and turned his back on me in a huff, not believing me, when I informed him it was against my religion to eat such food. I also took time to dutifully respond to letters from my friends. Christianne and I kept up a spirited dispatch which always concluded in her letters with the words "look out for my brother," whilst I sent her chocolates and coins in addition to pleasant words of my own.

Shortly after my letter-writing sessions, the lads and I would be called to partake in aviation exercises. Thanks to my experience from the aviation clubs back in Frankfurt, I have satisfied, if not impressed, my flight instructors here in the military with my command over the terminology and basic knowledge of aeronautics. Alas, however, it was as though I had to unlearn and relearn all my practical skills over again, this time behind the controls of an Albatros B.I, a very different craft from the civilian aeroplanes I piloted. Only in their first year of service, they made smashing reconnaissance machines, and we practiced day in and day out piloting the craft and providing a steady platform, that our observers might take photographs of our own lines; we didn't want to tempt conflict by snapping photographs of the enemy's. It was challenging work, but gratifying and, dare I say, entertaining, to zoom above the countryside and watch our men on maneuvers as our cameramen made certain to take pictures of the landscape below. With the urgency of our training missions hammered time and time again into our heads, it is an exciting moment in history, and I am proud to be prepared to make a difference in the fight for our autonomy as Germans, even if some of my fellow pilots seem less than pleased with me. I can only hope that if war comes, that I make a good accounting of myself and change their minds, but more importantly, that the conflict at large be short and not particularly bloody. That will teach those annoying doomsayers!

Of course, if a real war were to come along, we would have to fly higher and better than ever before. Our officers roared at us to remember our training. "Do not relax!" they would cry as we made to take off, mission after mission. Before long, we were climbing at one-and-a-third meters per second to astounding altitudes, the better to learn how to throw off the aim of anti-aerocraft gunners. Cruising along at 105 kilometers per hour, we found it difficult to determine the range of our patrols before we crossed over into enemy territory. At one point in our training, my squadron mate, Adelheid, accidentally crossed over into Russian lines and was nearly shot down by a warning round fired across the bow of his machine. As this was the first time he, or indeed any of us, was ever fired upon, he returned shaken, his trousers reeking from turned bowels. Fortunately, it appeared our friend Nicky the Second, Czar of the Russian Empire, had no desire to fight us that day and did not press matters from his throne back in Saint Petersburg.

As our many empires grow with nary a sign of war, save for some rumblings of discontent from within Austria-Hungary—Serbian nationalists striving for their own country—I think on how my new homeland of Germany stands in alliance with the very people from whom I sought refuge. I am unsure how I feel regarding this matter. It has been three years since Mayor Lueger's death, but my impassioned side may not be able to forgive my birth nation for their recent crimes against my fellow Jews, whose population has been visited with many cruelties over the past decades, and indeed, millennia. Though my more logical mindset reasons that Austria-Hungary was an open-minded empire prior to the late Lueger's rise to power and may return to form, I could not overcome my feelings of suspicion as I lit the Shabbos candles this past Friday. Said suspicions were then confirmed when the rittmeister strode in on my ceremony. Smiling indulgently, an awkward manner with twitching ends showcasing his slightly mossy teeth underneath his bristling mustache, he then informed me in what I deemed as kindly a tone as he possibly could muster, "I am sorry, Herr Schaefer, but I feel you should know that if we go to war alongside the soldiers, sailors, and fliers of Franz Josef, I may have to ask you to cease being quite so open about your rites." He coughed uneasily. *Kaff kaff.* "Please understand that I have no issue with your activities, and that you may practice them yourself, but . . . try not to flaunt them, you understand? It is bad for morale."

Even as I shake my head in disbelief at the kowtowing Germany does on behalf of their feebler brother-in-arms, I gloomily remind myself that I have made my choice to enlist in the military and shall stand by it. I *will* take great pains not to parade my Judaism. No longer shall I invite my fellow pilots to kindle the Shabbos lights alongside me, which has previously captured the interest of a few fellow intellectuals by birth but is deemed largely uninteresting by others. So as not to irk high command, I shall furthermore not lodge my request for leave to celebrate the upcoming Pesach Seder with my family and will instead observe the holiday by myself. After our past quarrels regarding the utility and service of Zionism to the Jewish community, I do not wish to escalate tensions with my family, and I do not wish to bring unwanted attention to my person. Perhaps in addition to being more subtle about my Jewish practices, I should probably attend the upcoming Easter festivities, as well.

As any good Christian pilot should.

30 June 1914

Disaster!

As I was standing by my Albatros, chatting idly with the ground crew after another uneventful but thankfully bloodless patrol, a courier came speeding in on a bicycle. He was wreathed in sweat and had peddled hard from Königsberg, spreading damnably tragic news. For all the anguish of the situation, however, I could not help but notice his handsome, honest, manly brow and spectacularly well-developed calves beneath his trousers. The man clearly was a master of his trade and very well-built. I then averted my eyes quickly as he caught me staring at him, politely inquiring, "Something the matter, sir?"

"No, no," I replied, blushing.

The courier smiled (so innocent and sweet, even in the line of duty!) before he brandished a telegram and thrust it into our superior's hands.

"Gentlemen! News from Sarajevo!" he cried.

"Why, where is Sarajevo?" one of our men said before scoffing.

Schilling silenced him with a withering look. He began to read the telegram. "Mein Gott!" the rittmeister exclaimed, doing a double take, then reading it again. "This may be it," he murmured to himself. "The war may yet come."

"Why, what is wrong, sir?" one of the burly ground crewmen inquired.

"Archduke Franz Ferdinand, one of our Austro-Hungarian fellows, has been shot in Sarajevo. Europe is abuzz, and we are behind in the times," Schiller said evenly. He looked down at us. "Politicians are attempting to muddle it out, which means they may turn to war at any moment." He chuckled softly at his own joke. "It is not likely, however.

In fact," he continued, "I am confident the whole thing will blow over. But if it doesn't . . . well, we will do our duty, of course."

You must understand, dear Diary, that if Austria-Hungary goes to war with what appears to be the Serbian nationalists who shot their archduke, Serbia, ever attempting to assert her independence from Austria-Hungary's influence, will be protected by their damnable big brother and our neighbor to the east, Russia, who will be looking to take care of the Slavic populations affiliated with her. This would include what Slavic peoples inhabit the Austro-Hungarian Empire. Germany, allied to Austria-Hungary, would be dragged, honor first, into the war and would almost unconditionally assist the empire of Franz Josef. If Russia and Germany join the fight, it is possible that other nations may follow. France is one such example, embittered by their lost land, now ours from the past war, as well as tied to an alliance with Russia. Regardless whether they or others join the fight, I am a pilot. I must do my duty. Fortunately, we are the kings of the battlefield and sky. Nobody would dare shoot at us beyond the occasional token artillery blast. Should I really be afraid?

Though I do not believe I shall engage in much combat, myself, the advance of technology on the ground is frightening. I do not know what shall become of my bosom friend Ludwig and his cavalry regiment, the Third Cuirassiers, who may well be called upon to charge into the teeth of machine-gun fire! When I retired to my rather cramped bunk later that night, I was quick to write by flickering candlelight a letter to him expressing my sincerest concerns to this effect, as well as remind him of my enduring love and admiration.

I wonder, too, how the citizenry will be treated if the Russians surge into East Prussia, or worse, even farther into the rest of Germany itself. I fear for my family, even for the senior aviators at the Society who snubbed me, and especially for Christianne. Though Christianne is working as a governess to the mayor of Königsberg, busy seeing to his many children, I hope she manages to one day see the world outside Königsberg and enjoy her life without war bringing the outside world to her.

27 July 1914

As I ran errands on behalf of the squadron today, I thought of Ludwig and his love of automobiles. I was able to drive a lorry to pick up beer for the squadron on their own dime. I've also been able to perform other odd duties amongst the community, including overseeing children at play within the Königsberg community.

Often when I fly just below the cloud cover, I can see the wonders of the earth below from my majestic height, and I notice the messengers, on bicycle and in motor cars. They look like little pinpricks! Truly, the bicycle messengers have gained their fair share of exercise over the past few weeks. Back and forth they ride. Back and forth, with news of imperial ultimatums issued and declined. I am glad I am not the one to invite the vitriol of their patrons by offering the dispatches they carry!

After a very patient month of allowing Serbian authorities to investigate the good archduke's murder in their own city, our allies have had enough. From what I have read from the papers and listened to from the lectures given by the rittmeister, Austro-Hungarian authorities, backed by our foreign office, issued a provision insisting upon allowing themselves to investigate the crime within Serbia. Serbia was also to be called upon to do its utmost to suppress further terrorist activities and their cells. All this seemed quite fair and logical to me, especially after the death of the archduke. Even the demand that Serbia cease spreading anti-Austro-Hungarian propaganda, whilst an impingement on freedom of the press, did not seem like a disaster, for who would speak ill of a country in mourning?

The Serbs, apparently. Hurtful and shocking. I never would have expected it of them.

And even if I did believe it unjust that our Kaiser Wilhelm backs Franz Josef wholeheartedly in demanding reparations that border on the extreme, and that our two factions have begun to enter into talks regarding military strategy in Potsdam (a tad strange, as the Kaiser did not even attend the funeral of the archduke and was said to have disliked him for his relatively leftist views), I cannot pity the Serbs. As I write, they, having shot the very Austro-Hungarian noble progressive enough to campaign for their rights, now appeal to Russia to stand alongside them in war on their behalf. I sit terrified, for if a war begins, we are sure to join our unlucky allies. Though a sort of righteousness could be seen for our side, as we only attempt to keep the peace, support the dealing of justice to the Serbian criminals, and honorably support the allies we went into this war with, it does not help that our strange bedfellows to whose defense we rush possess paper-thin defenses, composed of men of many ethnic backgrounds who are unable to understand each other. Lions though their soldiers may be, their officers might as well be deaf and as stubborn and incompetent as they would be asses as well.

All over the death of one man.

One can only hope that Great Britain will stay out of this war, but their perception that we intend to purposely put them out of business with trade and battle fleets of our own dies hard, and they are likely to take sides with France, Italy, and Russia if they are to be roused to fight at all. Saddening. Do not we, and not just Russia, have family members of King George V on the throne?

I must prepare to do battle, must practice my high-altitude photography, as I should learn both how to observe and fly. I should also write some letters—one to my parents, one to Christianne, and one to Ludwig. Though my mother has yet to write to me, I shall feel better having informed both her and my father as to the goings-on as I see them. It is a sort of moral high ground, I suppose, coupled with my sincere love for them and hopes that they stay safe in this time of conflict.

17 August 1914

Diary,

I awoke this morning to see my comrades in slow spirits. "Haven't you heard?" I was told by my portly, raucous, and uncomfortably blunt bunkmate, Flieger Erich Loessberg, when I inquired, "The Pope on his deathbed. Fever and lung complications seem to be the culprit. You should be in mourning."

"I should?" I replied. Caught off guard and perhaps rude in my response, but as that was his normal means of operation, Erich barely noticed.

"Ja, he was a Catholic . . . don't you Jews get along with them?"

I sighed, clapped him on the shoulder, and attempted to step away, before another pilot joined us.

"Nein," our rather short, frail, resident intellectual Catholic Tomas Fuchs shot back defensively, as though the thought of being my friend was abhorrent. "Spain's inquisition decimated their population there. Sorry about that, friend," he continued apologetically, before turning his sights on Erich again. "Yet Martin Luther was no fan of them either, hum?"

"No, sir!"

"Could you gentlemen cease and desist?" I replied testily as I threw on my leather jacket. "It pains me to hear of all the hatred you show my people."

"I mean, if you would just conv—," Loessberg began, but Fuchs silenced him.

However, even with the recent death of Pope Pius X, we of the FFA 10 have been instructed by high command to focus on only one thought that should cross the minds of us pilots of Germany.

That war is upon us.

After much preparation and many false alarms and heightened expectations, the game is afoot, and the first pawns of the Eastern Front have been moved.

Though the Russians have taken the initiative, we have seized the day.

The first day.

A small, boiling mess of enemy horseflesh was spotted today tromping across the Königsberg countryside by a fellow pilot-observer team some five days ago.

My homeland was under attack.

Perhaps not Israel, nor Austria-Hungary, but the one nation that has come to accept me in any sense.

Later that same day, as I was out on patrol, I too caught sight of the enemy for the first time at the fortunately comfortable perch of some six hundred meters.

Otto, my brilliant, sweet-faced young friend and botanist university student-turned-military observer, looked over the side of our craft with his camera lens, offering me a thumbs-up for providing such a steady platform. We noticed the large cloud of dust below us and, looking closer, saw thousands of horsemen probing the outskirts of Stallupönen. A solid brigade's worth. They moved slowly and were themselves just a scouting action (if one in force!), but off in the distance, I noticed at least ten times as many infantry behind them, with more in support.

More than I could even see, as their numbers melted into the horizon beyond!

An attack was on the way, and it had to be reported immediately. After my heroic observer waited, waited, waited, and then seized the perfect moment to photograph this vanguard, I swung my craft around as fast as I could, cringing as I heard loud creaking sounds coming from the wings. Praying in Hebrew under my breath, I eased up on my yoke and slowed my banking, keeping the delicate craft from breaking apart and returning to my base to report the advance of a corps numbering some twenty thousand. It was challenging to tell apart the men at this height, but with the assistance of Otto's telescopic-sighted camera and excellent skills, waiting for the perfect moment to shoot the film, we received a basic, but not comprehensive, understanding of what we were working against. Alarmed, I jumped out of my aerocraft and roared at my ground crew, awaiting orders and loitering about in the meantime, "Get this thing refueled and airworthy as soon as possible!"

The ground crew was initially less than helpful, disbelieving my claims when I first related the information.

"Well excuse me, King David!" one of them impudently replied. "We have no orders from flight command to do so!"

"Never mind that," I retorted, trying to ignore the jab at my faith and speaking as patiently as possible, though I was beginning to question my faith in these people. "This is a matter of utmost emergency! You! Inform the rittmeister! I'm going up again! I shall shoulder the consequences, myself!"

The mechanic brandished a wrench at me. "You'd better!" he replied.

Refueling myself by means of a quick, warming cup of coffee as my mechanics saw to my craft, I took flight again to determine a more exact number of those levied against us, whilst General von Prittwitz, Commander of the Eighth Army and our only hope against Russian invasion, was notified by telegram.

Striking out once more, the wings creaking with my every touch, we learned that there was even more from whence that initial force came. Not two, but four divisions—approximately forty thousand men, the vanguard of what must have been two hundred thousand men made up of cavalry, infantry, and artillery—were at arms against us. Upon once more returning to headquarters, I again breathlessly related my findings as Otto followed at a relaxed gait with photographic proof. After my superiors considered the pieced-together evidence, I was later notified in the mess by an ashen-faced commandant of the bad news: "Well done, flieger," he said, taking me by the shoulder. "Your service has been commendable. And yet, I must regrettably inform you that this is but one front of a two-pronged attack, the other discovered by your brother fliers." As I looked at him, horrified, he continued his report. "These are dark times, Schaefer. I must unfortunately conclude that we are very much wanting for men. Strung out as we are, our corps commander, Hermann von Francois, was delegated only eighteen thousand men with which to protect our homeland." He saluted me. "Wish us luck. We are to attack with haste."

"Attack?!" I cried. "Our army will be bled dry!"

"They will never see it coming," the commander replied.

Well, *that much* was true. The attack was authorized, and we fliers were sent to find any holes in the enemy lines that could be exploited. After several hours of circling and enduring potshots from below, we had no luck, and I jumped at every shot blasted in my direction. Clearly, this was no longer basic training! Otto, too, was all but frozen up, the young college boy shaking in his seat, gripping his camera tightly, but, like myself, resolute in his duty, however distasteful it may be. By the time we returned, crestfallen, to friendly territory, I clearly noted von Francois's troops already on the march across the muddy fields, oblivious to the lack of exploitations in the enemy lines! Upset and fearing for my allies' lives, I refueled and jumped once more with dread into my craft, despite the stammering of the ground crew, to view the outcome of the attack. Much to my great surprise, our Greycoats took advantage of a brief respite in one of the four enemy divisions. As the foeman halted to take on food and water, resting as the rest of the Russian force moved forwards, our soldiers slammed into them in a valiant, if somewhat outnumbered, frontal assault. In the intense fighting that followed, most of which I could not see from my altitude, the enemy had scattered to the winds! The view was glorious at a distance, so I flew in for a closer look.

With this Russian division having fled the area, I instead arrived only to watch firsthand the dead and wounded being shepherded away in a most tragic and heart-wrenching scene. Even as I sped by at a breakneck ninety-six kilometers per hour, the carnage was not lost on me. As I tried to regain my height and bearings, I surmised that we must have killed about a thousand and captured many thousands more. The hunched postures of the captured as they were led off was tragic, but there was no time to mourn them. At least the war was over for them.

The other divisions of our opposition scrambled to avenge their defeated comrades, blasting away at us with artillery, but by the time they had learned of their allies' plight, it was too late for them to make any real difference. A few half-hearted volleys later, the Russian guns fell silent for a time and the enemy, deprived of a choice position, was compelled to withdraw.

Having flown home and landed, Otto and I embraced one another, filled with many mixed feelings of regret and remorse at the cost of life on both sides, as well as satisfaction at a job well done and joy in our victory. We of the Central Powers have won a great battle this day, much to my sincere shock, but I wonder just how long we will last before we, like the Spartans at Thermopylae, are whittled down and die like dogs. The Russians' numbers are many, and though we inflicted massive casualties this day, if the enemy has any sense at all, our luck will not last. Perhaps we shall be reinforced, but unless drastic action is taken, Königsberg might fall after but a brief fight. This is why I was relieved to hear we were to withdraw to Gumbinnen after this successful repulse of the enemy.

I must admit, dear Diary, this is not the conflict I believed would never come. It is worse, far worse, than I could ever imagine, and I was a fool to think my homeland would emerge unscathed. I must write my mother and father at once to tell them to evacuate this land. Hopefully, reinforcements may come, or we can draw them into our homeland and beyond their supply lines so that we may destroy them or press them into a stalemate, though I do believe defeat may be a very real possibility.

I cannot write more on this topic. I must distract myself with a game of chess or cards, and fortunately, Otto has proven amenable to both, having been an avid gamer at university. Hopefully his command of gaming battlefields will contribute to that of real-life ones.

19 August 1914

For all my doom and gloom, our army, still flush with our successful delaying action over Ivan at Stallupönen, entertains a sense of renewed hope in the ranks of our imperial arms. Everything looks a little bit brighter for us, despite the grim reality of war, and whilst many appear disappointed that we did not defeat the entire Russian Army in one battle (it would have been ideal if we could have just talked it out), we are all delighted to still be alive. Here is hoping Nicky the Second's army does not reduce our smaller army to a quivering heap of bloodied flesh first.

I only hope I, alongside my friends, and indeed, even my "enemies" from other nations, can live to see an outcome. After today's scare, I am unsure this will be the case.

Having awakened early to the jarring of my alarm clock, I briefly conferred with the ground crew over a mug of coffee. "Careful out there, flieger," one said, adjusting his overalls. "I've been up for hours preparing your craft. The weather hasn't changed all day and doesn't look like it will do so anytime soon." He gestured out of the hangar into the blustery outdoors, where storm clouds had gathered. I was foolish and concluded with a shrug that these conditions were nothing I could not handle. "Thank you," I replied, "but I am sure I shall get along just fine." On that overly confident note, I took to the sky with Otto behind me, his camera clicking away like always, a smile upon his face. The wind was howling but made for an even more exhilarating experience as we ploughed through the sky and capered amongst the clouds.

Unfortunately, matters were about to change from exhilarating to petrifying. The weather took an adverse turn that was worse than our ground crew predicted. The clouds darkened only further and the winds picked up decidedly, buffeting our aerocraft. Soon, thunder sounded in the distance and Otto began vigorously tapping the side of our craft, indicating that he believed it was time to return home. Alas, it wasn't quite so easy. We had tarried far too long, such that even the Russians, suicidal in their bravery—or perhaps stupidity—did not themselves wish to take to the skies. As such, rather than be attacked by enemy aerocraft, we fell subject to assault by the weather instead. Lightning crackled around us, as the clouds began to open up and rain began to fall, forcing me to wipe my goggles clear of water with great frequency. Diving for home, my hands grew cold, even as I felt the heat from the engine. Then the heavens opened up and more thunderclaps sounded, growing ever closer to us. Or was that the sound of our plane breaking apart under the stress of the dive?

I managed to somehow guide the plane to a skidding, abrupt stop five yards from the barracks, after first landing on one wheel, then the other, before finally landing on both wheels on my second try. I immediately jumped from the cockpit and fell to my knees in prayer. Thank God for His preservation of my life and that of gentle Otto's! Otto, apparently not as fazed, lowered himself from the observer seat and patted me on the back comfortingly.

"Nice landing," he said consolingly.

"Perhaps," I replied mournfully, "but I never should have taken us up there."

From then on, I thought as I watched the ground crew snicker whilst guiding my craft into the hangar, *I will certainly be more discerning about flight conditions!* It was a truly terrifying endeavor, and one I shall do my utmost to avoid having happen again.

21 August 1914

They took Ludwig.

My heroic cavalier has at last fallen, and I could not even say good-bye. His death is unbearable to think about, yet it must be discussed, if only in some small detail, to do him some manner of justice.

What little sweetness in what victory we have previously tasted has turned bitter in our mouths, as the fates have turned against us.

What shall I tell Christianne?

I write hurriedly, having taken my meager dinner of cold chicken soup and rice back with me to my bunk, the food left over from the rest of my squadron's meal. I had arrived home late from the final reconnoitering of the day and am unsure of when my services will be needed next. However, I know that I shall soon have to watch powerlessly as my comrades fight for our lives against those who slew my much-adored friend. They never would have done so if they knew how pleasant a person he and the rest of us truly are, but now we must defend ourselves. I wish there was something I could do to raise everyone's spirits.

Suffice to say, a significant setback was suffered yesterday at Gumbinnen, but I cannot speak of it at the moment. For now, my thoughts turn to my beloved horseman Ludwig as I have returned from visiting the hospital. His breast pierced by enemy ordnance, he passed peacefully, under the influence of morphine and surrounded by well-intentioned doctors and doting nurses, but I remain inconsolable over the loss of good men, regardless of nation, in this war. *And to think it has only begun*, I ponder as I look disinterestedly at the bowl of rations provided for me. I cannot interest myself in partaking, yet nor can I force myself to sleep.

Today we suffered serious losses in battle, and though our future resistance, as with our prior endeavors, will be spirited, leading to only more bloodshed and violence, I see only a quick, bitter defeat or a long, hard-fought victory in the future. Having discussed this with my comrades, I was quickly hushed and told that if I felt we were on the verge of defeat, we had better not let the enlisted men hear of it. But how, dear Diary, I ask of you, can one be optimistic in a period of mourning one's best friend? And so many others besides? I contented myself with writing a letter of condolences to Christianne as I shakily murmured the Mourner's Kaddish under my breath, bending the tradition of my people. Perhaps she will understand the gravity of today's loss.

23 August 1914

Two days have passed, and I am still not myself, with the death of my beloved cavalier still constantly on my mind. It galls me that I cannot overcome this loss, but I shall forgive myself, as the memories we shared refuse to die. Tears well up in my eyes over the copious wine I imbibe as I drink toasts to his memories with my fellow pilots, however befuddled they may be. I can understand this. They do not know of Ludwig's valor and charity and, indeed, only care so much for the mysterious, somber Austro-Hungarian Jew, new to the squadron.

For a Jew I am, and not a terrible one at that, considering my surroundings. Jews are taught to question, to adapt, and not to lockstep at all times with all traditions.

Forgive my sentimentality as my tears stain your pages, o Diary. I feel lanced through the heart and in great pain at the loss of my allies. It appears everyone else exposed to the battle and its outcome has been pained, as well, and is shaken from the affair. Ever the empath, I feel their emotional traumas, and have had difficulty keeping myself from throwing military protocol to the wind, clapping the brave men on the back and offering them a cigarette. Nonetheless, I will attempt to retain a sense of decorum. I am a flier and outrank the common soldier in social circles. We must uphold our sense of honor, and it would be untoward of me to consort with such people. I have settled into my new headquarters along the Vistula River, taking up residence in a small barn. It reeks of horseflesh, reminding me all the more of Ludwig, and, though unable to grant me shelter from my sadness, it provides, apart from a slightly leaky roof, some coverage from the elements as I sit with a chicken leg, comforted only by a bottle of wine, which I use to toast the defeated and fallen, yet again, as the rain plinks off the helmets of our beaten army. They are embarrassed by another withdrawal, but are proud, and will fight again.

I must change the subject, lest I forever be bogged down in the cruelties of fate.

Diary, I shall discuss my observations of the war so far, instead.

It is clear that haste, even more so than Austria-Hungary herself, is our ally in the war against Russia. The foeman is poorly organized and undersupplied, despite their great numbers, and we are sure to win battles if only we strike quickly and decisively before the enemy can think and maneuver accordingly.

That is, if we maneuver wisely.

This past battle, I arrived at the mess to overhear that General von Francois, emboldened by our stand against all odds at Stallupönen, convinced General Prittwitz to take the lead in attacking the enemy again, all but neglecting their superior numbers. "He seems to be suggesting that we soldiers of East Prussia would be demoralized to leave our hometowns to the enemy, and thus will risk our unbalanced odds to steady the line," my fellow pilot, Kurt, remarked, poring over a newspaper in his hands.

"He might have asked us first," I responded softly, half-jokingly. It is true. Now, we are yet again stuck in a hastily conceived battle, all whilst obeying to the letter the borderline suicidal orders of Helmuth von Moltke, chief of staff of our nation. And though I love my family and Christianne and wish to fight for them, I do not wish to place them in trouble by putting my homeland in the front lines.

Nonetheless, I understand the logic. Moltke is doing his best. According to gossip in the ranks, he has entertained the insights of many other officers and constructed a reasoned plan to protect our nation. For the purposes of this war, this coalition has ruled in favor of adopting a defensive position with a small force along the French border. After all, we have liberated our own people of Alsace-Lorraine from France's grasp in recent wars past. Need we do more against these foes?

I also hear that reinforcement to the Eastern Front is on the way, and that high command shall ship a large portion of our soldiery stationed near France eastward to join our embattled men here in the East, as well as alongside our weaker Austro-Hungarian allies. Though Moltke had passionately argued for an attack on France through Belgium, all whilst committing to a holding action against the Russians, he has been over-ruled and has complied in the face of overwhelming pressure to push against the Russians and hold against the French. This is presumably to ensure the British, closer to the French than the Russians in friendship, move more slowly, if at all, to react to our maneuvers.

Despite the superior numbers of the enemy, we knew their disposition to be exhausted and depleted, and we were all optimistic about our chances.

How wrong we were.

Having discussed these depressing matters enough, I now feel at ease enough to depress myself further in recounting the fateful battle in which Ludwig fell.

It was 20 August. From our position in Gumbinnen, we saw a Russian force and moved to engage. They came in pieces, with dark clouds presaging their advance. First came the skirmishers, the Russian horse and cannon against our infantry, both sides fighting bravely through the corpses of their own men toward dubious ends. They inflicted many losses upon our good boys, but suffered, according to mounted scouts on our side, an astonishing five hundred themselves. This heavy loss of precious horse and manpower forced their withdrawal even as they pushed our men back.

Upon hearing of the engagement later that day, we pilots took to the sky, intent on observing the enemy from the cover of the clouds, dipping out of them once in a while to take photographs before dipping back to safety. Before we could finish our reconnaissance mission, however, I recognized, to my horror, that von Francois had begun his assault with his First Infantry Corps, backed by the cavalry under which Ludwig served. Clearly, they had hoped to set off in pursuit of what they construed to be a beaten army.

Diving low from the clouds, I saw Ludwig at his command position at the head of his crested-helmed cuirassiers. They had begun their charge against the enemy artillery, who put up a spirited resistance, saturating the cuirassier's battle lines with shell as I flew overhead. Unfortunately for the Russians, they soon ran out of ammunition and were again driven back. By the early afternoon, the enemy was assuredly on the run, suffering a nearly ten-kilometer retreat. Unfortunately for us, waiting for them was the stability and morale-raising reinforcement of a great many more Russian troops, prepared to spring to their aid. As I saw them move at a quick march onto the field, I could tell that trouble would follow, but was of course unable to exhort the cavalry to retreat. It was the Mosin-Nagant rifles of these Russian reservists that claimed gentle Ludwig's life. Though I could not ascertain the killer, nor did I see Ludwig struck down, nor could I blame them, I suppose, as both sides were called upon to kill the other. Nevertheless, I felt it in my bones as the Russian newcomers turned the battle from a rout to a stalemate, blasting away at our cuirassiers and later, straight at my own craft, forcing me to turn tail. But cruel fate would not leave us to this miserable outcome, instead resolving to worsen it, for then we were hastily routed, ourselves when our infantry were marched at the double-quick into battle against the now well-entrenched, reinforced, and adequately supplied Russian troops and guns, who promptly turned our flank. Curse General Mackensen's tardiness and the damned fellow who took sweet Ludwig!

Upon learning of this horrible loss as casualty reports and stretchers flowed freely, I shakily moved to return from my quarters to the hangar, where I was almost at once called upon to take to the sky again. This time, I was to withdraw from East Prussia altogether. "Telegram from high command," Schilling called out to the assembled pilots curtly. "The general would have us retreat yet again. We are to fall back to our aerodrome at . . ."

But I wasn't listening. Abandon our positions and our homes? To the Russians? What about our families? Fortunately, despite the distraction in my own mind, perceptive Otto, who had provided a small meal for me in the meantime, had marked the new aerodrome on a map, and, with some muttering and many tears shed by myself and my squadron mates, we flew off toward our destination, my plane shuddering from the many bullet holes the Russian riflemen had put in it. My heart was heavy to see my homeland sacked. I wept, watching our once proud army, now in ruins and mob-like in its disorder, making tracks for our new base of operations.

Today, however, I will no longer curl up upon my pallet of hay and cry once more for friends lost. I have drunk enough. As I realize the importance of controlling my impulses and staying focused in my endeavors, I conclude I am no longer to be a spoiled child. Whilst I cannot take matters such as this war into my own hands alone and must remain logical and philosophical, I can still reconnoiter the enemy lines and ensure that my comrades will suffer fewer losses. Though even as they brutally sack East Prussia, I cannot give myself away to hatred of the Russians. War, I suppose, is a dirty and in this case necessary business and I will do my job.

30 August 1914

As I slowly attempt to overcome my feelings of loss and grief over Ludwig, realizing that war will bring many more losses on both sides before it is done, I conclude that he would not want me to mourn, and would likely prefer that I not falter in my courage, so I shall focus upon the task at hand.

With this belief firmly in mind, I hope Ludwig can peer down from Heaven to see the Russians run, dear Diary. Even as I do not care to see pain and suffering, and I'm sure neither did Ludwig, I imagine he would feel vindicated to see those he would deem his foes driven from his home. It was horrifically violent and bloody, but at least seemingly decisive. The enlisted men and pilots alike call it a Sunday miracle, as the goyim believe the holy day of rest to fall on said day and not Saturday. Nonetheless, a miracle is a miracle, and I am willing to accept such a solemn, but important turn of events regardless of the day of the week. It was a day to be remembered, here on Tannenberg's blood-soaked fields.

To backpedal a few days, as we were called upon to retreat across the Vistula River after our botched attack at Gumbinnen, the Russians, perhaps wise to our plan, blocked our expeditious withdrawal, terrorizing us as they advanced ever closer. It was unseasonably cold the night before, and I had to sleep shivering inside a secondary bedroll I never thought I'd have to use but brought just in case and to appease Christianne, who had knitted it for me in a great act of needless generosity and adoration. Such affection was ill-placed, I fear, as I am nothing wonderful, but I wanted to be gracious for the kind gift.

Regardless, with the fate of Germany lying on our shoulders, we were forced to face our enemy. We fliegers took to the sky and began our scouting missions, but as we did so, we found ourselves making contact from another flank. Swooping low, I saw they wore the grey coats of Imperial Germany!

Allies!

Von Scholtz's Twentieth Corps, a diminutive force that was heavily outnumbered by the Russian Army, had nonetheless conquered their fears and taken the field.

The enemy force comprised five corps and a cavalry division—which my comrades in aviation and I saw bearing down upon our lads' position. Alas, our own force was flat-footed and von Scholtz's brave battalions were the only ones left to stand against the Russians' rapid advance. As the enormous czarist force snaked across the countryside, I felt ill, a sense of creeping doom in my stomach as I counted their men. We had faced off against the impossible before and prevailed, but to cheat defeat against such numbers . . . could it really be done?

General von Hindenburg, new to replace Prittwitz and to command us, seemed to think so, and his word was his bond. A bond that we had pledged to follow.

I took a quick repast to have a meager breakfast between flights. I am sorry, God, but I did partake in bacon alongside my eggs. The cruel cook who'd insisted for quite a long period that I should be ingesting pork like my fellow squadron mates served me the meal, and I was distracted by thoughts of my coming flights. Whilst I found myself slowly coming to enjoy the unique taste, the later assault on my stomach brought enough regret that I'm sure that will be the last time I try it. I would not be surprised if that physical response was a result of divine intervention for having tasted forbidden foods, even accidentally.

Despite retching from my body's attempt to adapt to the effects of ingesting a new food, Otto and I took off into the early morning skies of Tannenberg. Beauteous as they were, we prepared once more to risk our lives in desperate search of an opening in the Russian forces' lines that would grant an advantage to our own infantrymen and cavalry forces.

The enemy was not pleased to see me and met me with a hail of bullets as I passed by. Clearly, they were nearly as desperate to hammer home their last victory as we were to deprive them of these successes. Even the pilots of their observation machines stopped what they were doing and rudely attempted to fire on me with their pistols, issued for self-defense on the ground, not for an aerial assault! I cringed and weaved as a few glancing shots ricocheted off my craft and individual bullets embedded themselves in my tail, narrowly missing the struts of my aeroplane. Otto the observer returned fire with a pistol of his own, resulting in a great racket but no real damage. This, I wonder, may have contributed to our eventual victory, as their machines were tied up trying to bring me down, rather than scouting our lines for an advantage.

Unfortunately for them, not only did they miss their opportunity to note our flanking actions below, but my fellow fliers and I escaped with a passing knowledge of their maneuvers as well, noticing a gaping hole in the Russian left. It seems the enemy failed to keep cohesion as some elements advanced more quickly than others. Feeling dangerous this day, knowing I would be deeply troubled if Russia were to continue to occupy our lands, I flew low, only a few hundred meters, to better scope out the area with the secondary purpose of further riling up the enemy. I looked for the First Russian Army in vain, only catching sight of the Second Army and assumed the former would hold their newly won position at Gumbinnen and possibly leapfrog with their brothers following a victory here.

It was time to deprive them of this smug sentiment.

Flying home to the new, makeshift aerodrome, little more than a few small rickety shacks strung together, the airfields interrupted once in a while by refugee wagons ambling by, I immediately submitted my report to high command, impatiently waiting at their desks, as they pieced elements of a plan into place, and, after a bit of debate and discussion, Mein Gott did they have one. The isolation of enemy forces was key, and since our soldiers were able to find a copy of a telegram from enemy high command on the person of a Russian officer in an earlier skirmish, Hindenburg seemed quite secure in his decisions of maneuvers to come. So as not to bore you with specifics, o Diary, I shall say that the whole affair concluded in a bloody massacre. For better or worse, we won handily, taking many prisoners, and losing a rather small fraction of the force the Russians did. The enemy was repulsed, and is that not what matters most to the generals?

I fear so. The dearth of humanity in this world is galling.

This war is a clash of nationalistic values, which saddens me, but when the lives of those you know and love are on the line, certain deeds must be performed. This war has gone from a limited skirmish in the Balkans to a widespread conflict. I suppose we must protect ourselves!

And so we did. I now observe, dear Diary, that perhaps you are interested in the affair at Tannenberg. Very well. For posterity.

The Russians saw our buildup on their left, but took time to respond to our eventual attack, and even as they contributed cavalry from their first army (as the rest of said army waited for resupply), the ground forces were said to have given them a sound thrashing, throwing them off balance as we bloodied their wing, from which side *they* were supposed to attack!

Simply put from there, as our cavalry hid our numbers and maneuvers whilst slowing the supporting First Russian Army's advance, we managed to envelop and all but destroy the Second Army, capturing many tens of thousands and killing many more whilst their reinforcements still lay some sixty kilometers away. At the battle's end, we lost scarcely thirteen thousand men, whilst the enemy lost well over ten times that number.

It was a masterful ploy, however grim, and necessary, worthy of Waterloo or Austerlitz. Whilst I would normally never take joy in the killing of anyone, even I realize that it is a means to the end of survival of a war they encouraged and all but started. Even as I contribute to the deaths of thousands of individuals supporting so tyrannous and cruel a regime, I *still* would not exactly consider myself proud to have assisted in this butchery. They were pawns, and probably conscripted pawns at that, when it would be far more appropriate and helpful to the masses to topple the Czar himself. Still, at least I did not do the killing, and can relax, knowing that I had the honor of working alongside the likes of Hindenburg and saved the country, as well.

For now.

I also fear the day may come when I am able and, indeed, perhaps called upon to directly partake in battle from the cockpit of my noble steed. As many have already suggested, if the ground cavalry can enjoy such a combative pursuit, why cannot the knights of the air?

5 September 1914

Even as the Russians continue to ship more and more men to the front, the tides of war, for now, are seemingly once more in our favor. As we battle the enemy piecemeal, the citizenry of East Prussia made to return to business as usual, attempting to return to their normal lives and repair the havoc caused by collateral damage to their homes, fields, and businesses.

Papa's cheese business has remained mercifully physically unscathed, it was reported, though it looks gaunt and unwelcoming, surrounded by the burned and bombed-out remains of some of the other buildings around it. Upon his return from Berlin, where he stayed at a hostel for a time with Mother, Papa, visibly shaken, with many more white hairs in his beard, has come to visit briefly at our base on the outskirts of Königsberg. This was an exciting moment to savor, because it seemed to me as though he might have forgiven me for my eschewing the business world and our culture in favor of joining the air corps. For a time, we stood together in awkward silence, eyeing each other warily. His foot shifted, my eye twitched, and a moment later, we were both in tears. We embraced lovingly, and, as we wept, we recognized at once each other's intent and, like men, steadied one another and began bringing one another up to speed with matters of home and of war.

It is clear Mother thinks of me every day, Papa reported, but she is leery of bringing it up, as she is still upset that I would subject myself to conflict for any nation that may well turn their back on us at any time. As for Papa, he is more open-minded, and admitted of his own volition that he is "somewhat proud you would give back to a nation that showed us clemency and sanctuary. I respect your love of this nation, and you have made clear your patriotism toward it, which has indeed done us a good turn. Truly do you deserve the future of Germany, and they deserve you."

Over in his world, Papa reports that cheese continues to be in some demand, but customers and resources alike are dwindling with the French Navy's attempts to raid our ports and ravage our shipping. Though their forces at sea pale in comparison to the might of our greater navy and would be unable to stand up to us in a straight fight, their unorthodox sailing and guerrilla tactics force us to disperse our fleet and, as such, render us unable to successfully protect all our mercantile vessels. This, my papa proclaims, has brought great financial woes upon the family. "In addition," he continued, "Mr. Becker has suddenly taken ill, and it would be neighborly of you to show some support, as well." I bade myself to remember to send a card to Christianne and to her father, expressing condolences on this matter, even though the fellow, for all his efforts at attempting to repay me for saving his life, has ever resented me for being the blood of my parents, a Jew. I hope Christianne is safe, for one cannot possibly be well in the face of an ill father, a recently deceased brother, and a hometown invaded.

As the day marched on, Papa and I went up together in my aeroplane as I gave Papa a taste of my life. We caught a glorious glimpse of the sunset before we turned around for the base and, in thanks for what he deemed a "jaunt for the ages," had some Italian pasta (the food of our so-called "enemy") with marinara sauce. This was a delicacy made all the better as he presented me and the rest of the squadron with his entire current stock of parmesan cheese, secretly smuggled from Reggio Emilia in Italy and sprinkled upon our dishes! "Think of it as doing my civic duty, my son. God knows I have been shirking it too long," he said with a smile.

When the time came for Papa to leave, I told him to tell Mother I loved her, and that I missed them both. I then asked him to forgive me. "To my mind, there is nothing to forgive, my son," he replied. "As for your mother, she has already said the Mourner's Kaddish on your behalf. To her, as you are not a Zionist, you are an anti-Semite and dead to her."

7–8 September 1914

It appeared that our friends, the Russians, were on the run at last, forced back at Tannenberg by our superior scouting and communications. Alas, I was frustrated to find days later, in a flight over their lines, that though progress was made, the Russian withdrawal ended along the Masurian Lakes, bolstered by the XVI Corps, soon to be reinforced by the X Army. Stressed and exhausted by day after day of flying, it depressed me that for all my efforts, scores of enemy troops refused to be outdone and continued to advance on our position. "Will this never end?!" I shouted over the roar of my propeller blades as I soared through the sky and spotted them. It was as though our cause was hopeless. For all my genuinely peacefully inclined—if increasingly patriotic (though only for safety purposes)—tendencies, my rage was such that it was all I could do to not land my craft and angrily throw myself at the enemy on foot, seizing men by their shirts and shaking sense into them. Whilst I do not believe I would have been able to have made much of an impact as a single further soldier upon the ground, the concept of striking down an enemy has begun to seem gratifying if it meant a return to the status quo and a return to peaceful flight.

How selfish of me.

Perhaps, then, it was an auspicious change of fate when I went up this day. Flying above Russian lines to check upon the "barbaric invaders," as Schilling called them, I noted that reinforcements of our own had entered the field. With a leap of joy in my heart, I noted an additional force, the Guards Reserve Corps and XI Corps, marching along at a brisk pace to join our army from the Western Front. We had been briefed that they might do so, though they had travelled a great distance at short notice by railroad. Swooping low to salute them as they came by, knowing that their presence might mean a big push to press Ivan from our lands, I once more gained altitude, to better scout out the Russian forces and observe their lines, which were slowly linking up with their reinforcements.

Not high enough, it seems, in my overconfidence.

As I flew overhead, I was sprayed with a rain of machine-gun bullets that nipped at my plane's struts and fuselage, tearing great rents in my crate. *GOOD LORD!* I thought. *I have been hit!* I panicked and pulled too heavily on the ailerons and elevator, causing the former to snap off. Deeply troubled, I attempted to level out, my palms sweating, my brow veritably drenched, and my eyes welling up in tears, as I braced for a crash landing, desperately attempting to limp back to my lines with limited success. My machine dropped into the ground, crushing the wheels underneath itself, as my aeroplane proceeded to skid a good six meters toward friendly lines. The shock struck me hard as I fought to stay topside, leaning every which way to maintain some vestige of control as the wings of my craft shed under the pressure and scraping of the wayward fuselage. At length, gathering up my courage and equipment, I jumped, heart pounding, to safety from the skidding wreck, flames now issuing from the overheating engine. It soon met its end with a resounding explosion at the hands of a large boulder. Otto, my observer, was quickly engulfed in the flames. Noticing he was trapped in his observer station behind the cockpit, I quickly came to my feet and dashed back for him, but my run slowly turned to a walk, before I stood, frozen in fear at the sight of the flames. He died screaming in what must have been an agonizing death before I could gather my courage to rescue him.

By Hashem! The remorse I felt, and the sadness in my impotence! His screams would forever echo in my ears. The sight of me, unable to whisk him to safety from the hungry flames, but worrying for my own mortality, would haunt my dreams an eternity and a day. Shaking, I turned my head from this grisly sight to notice a great body of Russians thundering toward me. As they approached with their bayonets glinting in the morning sun, I prepared to meet death but, in a glimmer of rage, hoped to first avenge my brothers-in-arms, and, in a flash of motion, found myself with Luger in hand. Suddenly, a volley of rifle fire slammed into them as a regiment from the Guards Corps, fresh from reinforcing our lines, came to my rescue and carried me to safety. I was taken back to the base and told to rest a time. Thus had the battle of Masurian Lakes begun, though it ended for me noticeably early.

Though he may have been happy to see me alive, Rittmeister Schilling did not betray such sentiments lightly. "That plane was the product of much hard sweat and capital, Herr Flieger," the man intoned haughtily, turning his back on me with a swift pivot and click of his heels. "See to it that you are not shot down again. I will not have wastrels in my squadron."

"Jawohl."

Such were the only direct words I had had with the rittmeister in weeks. I had not time to even deliver my report! Schilling remained cold toward me, and when I rose the next day, expecting a new craft, attended by crews at the ready, I found none waiting for me. Indeed, the flight had taken off without me.

I was grounded.

It was a restless affair, being a pilot who had no aeroplane, no observer, but it made sense in a way, for though the war had just begun, all fronts were under great pressure and could not resupply their squadrons immediately. I paced endlessly across the airfield, attending the return of my squadron mates. The thought of Ludwig and Otto both dead weighed heavily on my mind. As I waited, I could not help but worry about the well-being of the other fliers. What if they suffered my very same fate? Or worse, death?

But no, they returned safely, and at Masurian Lakes the Russians once more took a beating, in part thanks to the intelligence we provided this day.

But what of myself?

"Reserve duties, Schaefer," Rittmeister Schilling commanded, almost apologetically, as he stepped out of his machine, riddled with shrapnel. "And you were right. It got pretty hot out there."

That night, I sat in my bed and, alone with my feelings, wept. Openly. For a time. As the tears ran down my stained visage, however,

I concluded that there was nothing I could have done to help. Otto could not have possibly known that, but had he done so, he would have understood. He would not want me in tears, either way, for it would only lead to the deaths of more of our brothers-in-arms. I felt a little better for a time and managed to sleep the rest of the night. But the next morning I received news that shook me to my core.

Italy, Russia, and France had all signed an agreement which insisted none of them sign separate peace treaties with our nation. In one stroke of a pen, this war had become a bitter fight to the end.

17 September 1914

We pushed them back.

The Russians, praise God, are beaten and in full retreat from East Prussia, off German soil at last.

Though I could only experience it by binoculars from afar, the lads did well—that is, they succeeded in killing many, as we cemented the defeat of the enemy army, soundly thrashing them for what must be the last time on our Eastern Front.

Surely it was?

It was, either way, truly a day to be grimly satisfied with our achievements, but not a time to be smug. Not only did these victories cost countless lives on both sides, but, whilst we focused on our own defenses, our "allies," the Austro-Hungarians, were unable to defend their own lines nearly as successfully when the Russians smashed into Galicia. There was a lesson to be learned in all this for the future: one cannot assume the Austrians can hold the line alone!

As if that was not terrible enough, our own victory in East Prussia involved redirecting forces from the Western Front to even the odds as Russia sent army after army to confront us. The result of our costly win on the Eastern Front also resulted in a bloody but determined French offensive that nearly pushed us out of Alsace-Lorraine! As Pierrot, the bitter and duplicitous Frenchman, continues to forge ahead toward Berlin from the west, it is clear to me that our redirection of the Guards Regiment from the Western Front might well have contributed to our woefully thinned line in that region.

Fortunately, the men of the Western Front were about to get a bit of assistance.

Mine.

With the transition of new pilots to our squadron, alongside their machines, there was little room for me to be present without one. I was thus transferred to the Sixty-Second FFA, who were quartered at an air base in the far eastern region of Alsace, specifically, Strasbourg, on the Western Front. There, I do believe I shall repay my fellow Germans for their valiant defense of my homeland in East Prussia by aiding them in pushing back the French blaggards who dared ally themselves to the Russians and, less than half a century ago, opposed our very unification in the first place. I shall count this as a victory, as I did not really get along with anyone here and may benefit from the change of scenery, if not the loss of easy contact with family.

Who also seemed to not care for me.

The men of my old squadron promised to write to me frequently, referring to me time and time again as a bosom friend and hugging me tightly in never-ending embraces. Though I knew better than to take their promises at face value, I could tell that my skills had left an impression on them. This was satisfying. Though I was lonely and isolated, perhaps to an extent of my own doing over the course of my stay with them, I had gained their respect.

Mission accomplished.

We took one last meal together in the creaking, old, rather woebegone barn of a mess hall. Comprising pork, beans, and lager, it was a simple but tasty meal (however sacrilegious), but all we had, and I would remember it well for its bittersweet nature more than for its quality—where was the cheese? Still, it was wonderful to dine with the men and bond at long last, however late it was in our acquaintance. We exchanged home addresses and expressed a desire to write one another further postwar. I am sure anyone I will encounter in the Sixty-Second FFA will be easier to get along with than Rittmeister Schilling, but it is a damn shame the others couldn't join me, I mused, as they escorted me to the train station.

5 December 1914

Ah, Diary! I thought I had lost you, but it appears that I should merely check the inside of my newly issued AEG observer more thoroughly. Though a smaller craft than that which I used out east, it is faster and has so far proved more successful in the accomplishment of missions. This is of great use, as we are up against quality, not numbers, on this front and may be in for a very difficult war. Indeed, with Moltke's new plan to dig in defensively to stymie the British war hawks clamoring for their nation's entry alongside France, I see our hopes of a speedy victory in the west flickering. It had best not be a sign of times to come. Fortunately, with our triumphs over the Russians on the Eastern Front, we might soon band together with the Austro-Hungarians and drive the Russians from Franz Joseph's lands as well, throwing Ivan on the defense. This is good timing, because the Austro-Hungarians, though not as skilled at war as we, have taken Belgrade, the capital of Serbia, in a bloody display of arms. This victory would have been fairly decisive had the Austro-Hungarians been able to keep the war local, but alas, things always seem to be complicated by the advance of time. Serbia is now a minor power in the overall struggle and this conquest will do little to sour the taste of war in the mouths of the French, Russians, and Italians.

In other news, there is much to love about my new squadron, the Sixty-Second FFA. First off, the lodgings are far superior to some of my past aerodromes. It is attached to a most pleasant and rather well-run small farm which provides us with fresh eggs, and is on the outskirts of a lovely, rather large city, thankfully somewhat untouched by the war and with tasty fare to be found within. Despite the aforementioned wear and tear on the surrounding towns and the understandably sullen moods of the citizens, we can always smell the baked goods from the boulangerie not far off, which is happy to sell to us at wildly increased prices, seeing as we are on what was once French territory, only recently occupied by our men. Nonetheless, we pay these prices, rather than ransack the shops, because we are men of honor. We hope the war will end soon, and we want everyone to be on as reasonable terms as we can be.

On that note, the pilots are likeable rogues, quick to crack a joke or a bottle of liquor with equal likelihood, and none more than the rotund, soft-spoken, and understanding Rittmeister Kurt Muller, mother hen to the squadron and the only flieger not possessed of facial hair. Truly am I blessed to have such an understanding commander, who was quick to treat me to some excellent sausage and brandy. By this point, I had found the flesh of pigs a commonplace taste. Only after the meal was complete did the rittmeister take me up in his personal machine to acclimate me to the battlefields I was to scout. "For who," said he with a warm smile, "could scout on an empty stomach? Never forget to dine well before you head out, flieger. It may be your last meal!"

Bounding along at 110 kilometers per hour, I found what was left of the French countryside quite beautiful—it was a shame that it was being steadily reduced to a sea of blood. Shell holes and trench lines everywhere. It was my responsibility to see the war to a quicker ending, and that, I solemnly pledged, I would do, for the good of all peoples.

Also of note is Fischer, chief mechanic for the squadron. He played an ingenious practical joke on me the first time I was acquainted with my own machine, slathering glue on the seat of my crate, sticking me fast to my observer chair, for this was the role I was to take in my first jaunt up. As soon as I felt the fabric of my trousers ripping and the cool air whipping amidst my buttocks, I felt a degree of ire, certainly, but the invigorating wind and merry, rather than derisive, laughter of the mechanics put me at some degree of ease. I was amongst strangers anyway and did not wish to come off as a stick-in-the-mud, and instead smiled, at peace with their mischievous shenanigans. It wasn't long before a new pair of trousers were procured for me—their cost, anyway.

Compliant with this conspiracy was a very attractive gentleman pilot, a brooding beauty by the name of Fritz Weber. Leggy, with a long, thoughtful, attractive, and Byronic face to match—one that seemed as though he was silently bemoaning his lot in life and the war at large—it was he who was assigned to fly our curious contraption whilst I spied on the enemy. In the cockpit, it was revealed he was an ass with a heart of gold, and, though quick to ascertain my Judaic background by "a look at your curly dark hair and hooked nose," the remarks he made were clearly playful in nature, asking if we ate Christian babies and had horns. I took the inquisitions seriously, knowing that some of those overhearing did not know of my people and might be influenced, but jokingly lashed back at the loudmouth until we found ourselves faux dueling with a pair of riding crops appropriated from the stables, knee-deep in snow and having a grand old time, with me, thanks to Ludwig's tutelage, even carrying the fight before Muller restored order by accidentally (or so he claimed) emptying the contents of a chamber pot upon our heads!

They are a band of stouthearted pilots and crew, brave and true pioneers in their newfangled flying machines, but most importantly, they take to their travails with a gallows humor that helps them face the next day. I do believe I shall enjoy flying alongside these men.

10 December 1914

A most peculiar episode has come to pass as I navigated the Western Front, struggling with the camera as I played the observer role for the first time in my military career. I was reminded of Otto, the late observer for my own craft back out east and couldn't help but shed a tear or two. Though we did not know each other overly well, we were bound by the fires of war. He was a fine ally by merit of his patience, stabilizing smile, and our cohesive working relationship. It was a shame I did not appreciate the young, idealistic university student's skills earlier on, for he handled his camera expertly, despite my inexperience with the aeroplane model we were using.

The camera I was given to operate along with the Sixty-Second FFA was a clunky device and I had no idea how to use it until Weber, sighing good-naturedly and muttering, showed me how to operate the shutter. Though I once *shuddered* with indignity at the thought of myself taking a scouting photograph so far above the field of battle, I now truly grasp the difficulties of the art and show no great talent in using it. My first shots were absolutely horrific—blurry, blotchy messes that were useless for strategic planning, but with time and tutelage, they began to *develop*.

Ha.

It appears as though Weber's humor is wearing off on me.

I will always be thankful to Otto and Weber both for their introduction to this world. I promised myself to honor the life of the former by working hard to improve my skills until they approach his level, as well as Weber's level.

My time up as the observer, rather than the pilot, was curious. Seated behind Weber with the camera, I was shakily snapping photographs, as per my orders, when a great aeroplane came soaring into view, the roundels on its wings and fuselage a vibrant blue, white, and red from the center out.

"Frogs!" I did cry, remembering the lessons learned from the Eastern Front with Otto and putting aside the camera and going for my trusty Luger. Fortunately, my commander was quick to veer our vehicle off course and with it throw off my shot.

"Don't be a boorish barbarian, Schaefer," was Weber's laid-back reply. "That's Claude DuBois and his brother Renee. The two wouldn't hurt a fly. Nor would any other pilots on either side. Is that how you welcome our hosts? Show some respect!"

"Are they not our enemy, sir?" I replied, scarcely believing my ears.

"Indubitably, but they've never sought to strike us down. Why should we do so them?"

The man had a point. We were not paid to shoot the opposition, but merely to shoot photographs of the ground. Why endanger our own lives through engaging in the former?

I pocketed the weapon and waved instead as the brothers DuBois waved back. This was the kind of war I could get used to. If only others might follow suit!

25 December 1914

Yesterday proved to be yet another interesting experience, this much is for sure.

Christmas whilst at war.

Trees being felled with enthusiastic abandon.

Lights everywhere.

Carols being sung.

Turkeys being harvested for the slaughter.

It was an important holiday for those devotees of Jesus in our squadron—in short, all men except for me. I had no choice but to be swept up in the festivities. Why it is important to these fellows to celebrate the birthing day of one of my people so long ago in a locale so far from here, I'll never understand, but it was a welcome respite from my duties in the skies, entertaining though they have become.

I expected it to be a long slog, with me doing the work of the twelve pilots in the squadron whilst the others celebrated, but apparently, I was already made out to be their brother, having only flown with them for but a few months. As such, it was at their invitation that I came down to the officer's mess to enjoy a grand turkey dinner alongside cranberries and almonds, as well as apple pie and bars of chocolate. We gorged ourselves with some remorse, able to only wonder what miserable supplies the poor souls in the trenches were consuming at this time. Not wishing to bother them on this special holiday, fearing we might invite vitriol based around our different lifestyles, we instead appropriated a football from a local home and challenged the mechanics to a bout. Considering the brawn and coordination of the mechanics, we aristocrats did well for ourselves, but it was clear we were unevenly matched.

Fortunately, as the newest member of the squadron and a Jew to boot, I was not called upon to participate for our squad, but instead refereed, expected to know implicitly the rules of the sport, "as any true German is wont to do," the rittmeister remarked jovially.

Though possessed of only cursory knowledge of the sport, I refereed to the satisfaction of both sides, each participant knowing the rules well enough to police themselves passably. That did not keep the mechanics from slaughtering us, seven goals to three. The engineers returned to their quarters in fine spirits . . . and in possession of many bars of chocolate won off the pilots, much to the latter's chagrin. I was the only one to escape with my bar—the perks of being the referee, I suppose. I was, in addition, invited to the engineers' quartering house to enjoy the chocolate with them alongside cigars in commemoration of the holiday, and accepted with a smile. In doing so, I got to know our staff somewhat, which included a fellow Austrian of a somewhat pleasant disposition named Lukas.

A pleasant disposition but a very rude look. Mossy teeth, soiled overalls caked in engine oil, and a spotty face.

Introducing myself nonetheless, I was immediately recognized as "that Jewish pilot" and was of course made light of for a few moments before I was informed by Lukas most seriously how very sorry he was for the behavior of Vienna's Mayor Lueger. "You will have no trouble from my people these days!" he shouted jovially. "We now have nothing against the Hebrews!" I nodded, and to spare him the embarrassment, asked what brought him to our aerodrome. He replied proudly, "Horse theft!"

Even our tinkerers are a colorful bunch. I will take great pleasure in getting to know them more as well.

Despite this, it was a very spiritual experience to have our brave band of soldiers, engineers, and pilots alike gather around the Tannenbaum and sing carols, praising their Lord and Savior—a fellow who, even to my reckoning, was an upstanding individual, if not the Messiah himself. We Jews hold out for a greater man still than their Jesus, but it was nice to feel connected and be a larger part of something once more.

This time, I was for sure one of the team.

The week ended the next day with Fritz and me conspiratorially and puckishly smuggling a quintet of piglets and letting them run hog wild in the officer's barracks, having first numbered them one through six, leaving out the number three, in the hopes that the officers would be forever searching for the third pig. This was considered by my people to be a grotesque act, the handling of pigs, but it was such a brilliant prank that I let it go. Someone had to get back at the rittmeister for pouring the chamber pot on our heads that fateful first day!

3 March 1915

It was in the frigid cold of this day, staring grimly out the window of our barracks, that I feel today as though I have now lost hope for all humanity.

After observing for a few jaunts along the Western Front, I managed a sort of somatic signed language with some of the other pilots, and we were able to engage in basic conversation to pass the boredom of our reconnaissance patrol flights, as even the anti-aerocraft fire had become routine and failed to jostle me further. With my brotherhood of "flyboys" by my side, I have been able to breeze through the war for the past month or so. This war will certainly not end all wars, but at least I felt some camaraderie amidst the mechanics and pilots, the latter of whom—German or French—I have developed a great fellow-ship with. It was a far more civilized front than that of Eastern Europe, fighting alongside the Austrians and against the Russians.

It was because of this sense of brotherhood, I suppose, that I would never have construed the shrug of Capitaine Giraud of L'Aéronautique Militaire in response to my jovial wave one day as hostile until it was too late. Even as his observer, Caporal Clouseau, went for his weapon, I never saw it coming.

The first shot from his Lebel rifle went wide, but the second round hit the struts of our craft which supported the wings, causing our craft to wobble violently.

We were under attack!

Weber, shocked, threw our crate into a hard right bank with a loud swear, attempting to break for home. He had not expected this kind of duplicity either, but he was quick to recover his nerves as he gestured at me not to return fire.

I, however, panicking, misunderstood Weber's frantic signaling, and to see him so concerned fueled my own wrath. In a horrific and toxic combination of outrage at the Frenchmen's betrayal of the unofficial rules of war we fliers had established, as well as frustration that I am unsafe wherever I go, I felt myself at breaking point. I could take no more of this abuse, be it from civilians in my past life, soldiers, or even now my brother fliers, regardless of which front I fought from, and took another approach to the situation.

I proceeded to fight. As I once more went for my Luger, which I until all too recently thought would only come in use against the unwashed masses on the ground or against nature, I shakily aimed, guided by my anger, and fired a round at the offending observer, who ducked, and the shot whistled overhead. I grunted in frustration. It would have struck him had he just stayed still!

It was then that Clouseau made his move. Bounding upwards from his hunched position in the fuselage of his Bleriot reconnaissance craft, he fired once more with his longarm, aiming at Fritz, our dashing and fearless pilot! To the enemy's credit, it was a fine shot, as the rifle round blew a hole through Fritz's shoulder, defying even his heavy winter coat!

God! No!

Badly injured, my companion slumped over the cockpit controls as the plane began to plummet downwards. The situation was nothing like, yet still related to, what happened with Otto, and if I did not act, I would have another dead body on my hands. As the enemy contraption peeled off and made for their home base, assuming us undone, I managed to rally Fritz through his pain. "Weber, please. Do not fail on me now! We must dash for home at once. We'll see you through this!" I cried, shaking him into lucidness. Nodding weakly, our heroic pilot once more seized command of the crate. Fighting what was clearly considerable agony and some structural damage to our machine, he eased the controls backwards and guided the aeroplane's nose upwards ever so slightly as it descended, performing a textbook emergency landing in a field a mere kilometer behind no-man's-land on our side and mere yards in front of a startled farmer. "Please, a man needs your help!" I shouted in German at the befuddled farmer, but he was too shocked to respond. Upon guiding him to Fritz's body, now bleeding out, the poor beleaguered laborer shook himself and ran inside to call the local doctor. It was a torturous wait of forty-five minutes before the physician arrived, and in that time, Leutnant Fritz Weber was beyond hope. He passed in considerable pain, the rifle round having caused him to bleed out despite our best efforts to staunch the wound.

It was then that I lost much of my fervor for peace. The death of so many ground troops was tragic. There was Otto, and now Fritz too?

I swore an eternal revenge against Clouseau and Giraud for starting what I assured myself was the first of many duels to come. My thoughts only returned to the deceased himself later in the evening, when a solemn funeral was held for our companion who had died so needlessly.

I must be cautious, for I could be next. These were the words I thought as I stood amongst my fellow pilots the next day, when we were lectured about the recent affair, hammering it home only further into my head as my mind swam with the memory of my lost comrade and the terror of the encounter. Thus, as my fellow pilots, in sympathy, bought me dinner at a nearby café and took me out to the moving pictures, specifically an American film called *A Fool There Was*, which was about a family man who is seduced by a psychic vampire, I was hard-pressed to comprehend anything more about the film in my haze. I could not help but utter distracting thoughts of hopelessness and terror, having seen so many good men on the ground and in the air die, and almost certainly came off overly gaunt and grim, ruining the party in Fritz's honor. I felt bad, but it was also reflective of my innermost thoughts. We are at war, not a sporting event, and, as much as I hated this fact, I had to internalize it.

5 March 1915

Having been given a day to mourn, I took to the sky once more today, 5 March, with one sordid goal in my mind. It was a far cry from my normal mindset, but then, war brings about all manner of unnatural feelings.

Or were these feelings natural, and the feelings of peace and kindness used to unnaturally condition us to ensure the continued existence of man?

Whilst there was no doubt that observing would be done, and that we had to acquire accurate information about enemy entrenchments and positions along the Western Front, I decided it was very important to make a personal matter of Fritz's death.

Otto's as well.

I would bring down an enemy aeroplane. Perhaps one for each. It was not a pretty thought, and I could feel myself second-guessing my every action, but in the end, it was a matter of honor and necessity.

It was Fritz, after all, whose humor enabled my acceptance in the squadron, who performed so many silly pranks in goodwill. Who taught me the rules of chivalry in the skies and who died attempting to adhere to them.

Whom I secretly very much admired, and perhaps not only platonically.

Though in hindsight, perhaps he would have preferred his young charge not be corrupted by the behavior of others; I have become consumed with rage, followed by a need for revenge.

Today, I found it.

Flying high above enemy lines with my new pilot—a tall, bony, silent fellow who was, in fact, true to his personality, a descendent of that self-same Grimm family that united Germany in its adoration of their folk-tales—I encountered anti-aerocraft shells bursting all around us, but found nothing of too much interest to report on the ground. What was worse for me was there were no enemy planes to target, at least at first.

Grimm had given me a talking-to on the matter. "Focus on the mission, observer," he had remarked when he caught me dragging a Mauser infantry rifle on board our aeroplane. "Your single-minded pursuit for revenge will be our undoing, and that of Germany's in addition. We have lost a comrade, true, and of course I mourn for him, as do you. But would he want us to escalate the war and bring it to the air, merely because of one instance? The infantry lose far more than one comrade every day. What gives us the right to complain more than they, the poor fellows who are bombarded by artillery, charged by cavalry, and shot at and strafed by rifle and machine gun from land and above?"

He was right. I knew it. But it was easy for him to say—he hadn't had a trusted accomplice and, dare I say it, infatuation, killed before his very eyes. His speech didn't keep me from hauling along the piece. I knew it flouted our code of conduct in wartime to use such weapons from the air, but they had initiated the air war, and I could not allow myself to be bullied by the opposition as well as by my own side.

The rifle would suffice, but at what target would I vent my wrath?

The answer came swiftly to me as Grimm and I turned for home, having photographed our targets on the ground. Blocking our path once more were the valiant DuBois brothers, jovial as ever in their flailing hand signals. Alas, every signal they threw at us only increased my outrage. I reached for my Mauser, and began working the action on my piece, pulling back on the bolt of the weapon, feeding five individual bullets into the rifle before pushing the bolt forwards and locking it back into place. The weapon was then cocked and I next let loose and fired a 7.92x57 caliber warning shot.

Into the pilot's head.

The horror was palpable as his body slumped against the side of the fuselage, tilting the machine as the DuBois brothers' plane went into a nosedive. As the crate picked up speed, shedding its wings, I realized, as my passion subsided, that I had killed two unarmed men.

Though I could hear Grimm yelling at me over the roar of our engine, my mind was full of images, not words, as I stewed in the combined horror and glory of my first aerial victory—a pair of idealistic French boys enamored with the concept of knighthood.

For Otto.

I was a monster. But in a sense? Not to defend my acts, but the duties those boys were performing were necessary for the French war effort.

Was it not necessary to end this war as soon as possible?

I was a monster, yes, but my acts are a necessary evil.

It no longer pleases me, but I foresee this war escalating to the skies above and these engagements happening with great regularity.

I amongst the perpetrators.

10 March 1915

It has been five days since my first kill—one in revenge for the loss of my comrade, an affair for which I would have been awarded the Iron Cross, Third Class. And yet, so upset was Grimm that he refused to recognize the kill we received together. Without this recognition, the kill was not confirmed, and I was awarded neither the kill, nor the cross. I was furious! "I understand your upset feelings about me striking down the DuBois fellows, and I do not feel well about it myself," I remarked testily to him one day as we underwent kit maintenance, "but as a Jew, I need this recognition as a warrior!"

Either way, the war continues, and my desire for revenge has not been quelled in its entirety. What's more, conflict in the air has become a commonplace affair and I have become a target of the foeman for striking down their beloved fellows. Today, however, was especially terrifying, as I faced down a new obstacle to overcome.

Flying along the enemy front, collecting information to direct artillery fire (to be relayed once on the ground again), I chanced across a curious-looking plane with only one bank of wings. Hailing from a new squadron whose markings I couldn't identify, it posed a danger to us at once as it loomed ever closer. It possessed a Hotchkiss gun, primed and ready for action.

That is correct, dear Diary. A Hotchkiss gun.

Unfortunately, I did not see him until it was too late. He dove from the sun and came at Grimm and me at a frightening speed.

I had not been at the business end of a machine gun for some time, and certainly not one based on an aerial platform.

DAKKADAKKADAKKA!

"What the blazes?!" Grimm cried as he steered sharply, immediately aborting the mission and heading for home. I ducked into the fuselage for my rifle, newly authorized by Grimm as a necessity for self-defense "since you kicked the hornet's nest last mission," as the flurry of bullets rent holes in the wings and struts of our crate.

Another volley slammed into our craft, shredding our fuselage.

DAKKADAKKADAKKA!

I began to panic.

A bullet grazed my left shoulder, barely impacting against my fur coat, meant to combat the elements, in a very close brush with fate. The world began to get hazy and blurry as psychosomatic symptoms set in and my mind convinced itself that the round had hit home.

It would appear, in the long term, that I would be fine.

Not, however, if we were to be downed by this well-armed craft first.

As the plane swooped around for a final assault on our machine, I fired several rounds in an attempt to keep it at bay. It was to no avail, as it loomed ever closer.

Then it opened up on us again.

DAKKA–CLICK–DAKKA–CLICK–CLICK–CLICK!

The gun of the enemy vehicle had jammed!

As my vision continued to swim, I managed to load one last round into my rifle and fire it at the offending craft.

KRAK!

Praise be to God!

I managed to hit the propeller and the enemy disengaged, his machine damaged by my lucky shot.

Limping home, Grimm affected a bumpy emergency landing and reported our close brush with the foeman and the usage of a machine gun on board an enemy craft. Meanwhile, I was immediately seen to by our talented doctors. For all my fears, the wound was indeed super-ficial and posed me little threat, causing no end of embarrassment as I thought of how my vision had swum from a mostly psychological injury. We were told that we were not the only ones to feel the heat of enemy machine guns of late, but not to worry, that a craft was being devised that would respond to the power of the so-armed Morane-Saulnier Type N scout.

Here is hoping.

In the meantime, I counseled myself, I had to stop panicking in the face of injury, for if more machine-gun-wielding craft were to dominate the skies, I would have to learn to keep a cool head under pressure, even as their bullets struck my craft or even myself.

I am but an extension of the machine and pilot, and the three of us must act accordingly as a well-oiled, cohesive machine, with unshakeable precision and bravery.

17 March 1915

Pesach at last, Diary! Though I am not sure it would do to celebrate it too vocally here in the middle of Christian company. Much to my good fortune, however, the skies were quite cloudy today and I did not need to fly. Like my ancestors of old, I could relax on this most holy and fortuitous day.

Spending the morning slaving away in the kitchens like my ancestors of old in Egypt, I, much to the staff's curiosity, managed to prepare for myself a crude incarnation of unleavened matzoh bread. This ritual food, very much unlike the fluffy bread usually served to us, was consumed by my squadron alongside me with curiosity, alongside a supply of roast beef, which I acquired after a brief argument with the quartermaster down at the mess. I also took great pains to find some materials for a traditional chicken stock soup my mother was fond of making and that she had passed on to me as I reached adulthood. After adding matzoh balls to each bowl and uncorking a bottle of wine to complete my repast, I sat myself down in the parlor and pondered my people's predicament. Once slaves, we are now a scattered nation, a fate little better as we are a distinct minority in every locale we inhabit and an easy target for oppression just the same, as I have long known in my life. It is a strange thing, religion. A concept that brings out so much good in some, yet such ill in others. What with all the violence going on in the world in this day and age, it is also a challenge to conclude that a truly benevolent god exists, and, as I look down upon my empty bowl, once heaping over with soup, I find myself lonely in my religious postulations.

As I am at any other time of day.

I wonder how such an all-powerful creator could let us all come to harm.

But no. I have gone too far and said too much. This is not the talk of a follower of the Jewish faith, and I would not see thousands of years of my traditions and people trodden into the dust because of my queries.

Though then again, is it not my right, nay, my duty, as a Jew, to question?

4 April 1915

Diary, I have received an epistle over the past few days that has given me hope and a cause to fight for. It is in Papa's handwriting, informing me in short but loving language of his pride in knowing his son is an airman of Imperial Germany. He had heard through the grapevine of my valor and, whilst rejoicing in these actions, begged me to come home safely when the time comes and to fly with prudence in the meantime. He furthermore reported that Mother is well, and, whilst she curses my, to her mind, poor decisions, she too sends her regards. I related this news to my compatriots, who were delighted to hear of my good spirits.

Aviation combat is sparse, so I have not much of a chance to make a showing of my newfound vigor. Whilst I will not purposefully endanger myself, neither will I shy away from eliminating French aerial threats to the Fatherland. Not only does Weber deserve that I fight so diligently and with passion, but my home country does as well.

9 May 1915

At last, we have a weapon capable of breaking the enemy's stranglehold over the skies of France, and thanks to high command hearing of my valor against the Russians, I have been amongst the lucky few chosen to use it!

I have been transferred, just days ago, to yet another new squadron. This one is bent on a new goal. The orders of the Feldflieger Abteilung 6b, based out of the beautiful and recently constructed (still smelling of newly sawn wood, in fact) cornflower-strewn Bühl Airfield, near Sarrebourg, are simple. Rather than observe enemy positions and document them, we are tasked specifically with seeking out and destroying enemy observer craft responsible for the suffering of our men below, as well as defending our own observers from those set on knocking them from the skies.

We are a band of elite pilots who are prepared to serve the Fatherland with honor, and whose eagle eyes will spell doom for many an Entente pilot. I am morbidly intrigued to partake in this activity, however inwardly horrified, for though I know I am of use in an observer craft, whether as pilot or even photographer, I felt it necessary to prove my utility and loyalty as a representative of my family and people to that of Father Germany in whatever way they need me, and thus must continue to be a killer as well. As an observer, I was worth something, but now I can do so much more. Between actively shooting enemies from the sky and depriving their armies of information, I can at last be a knight of the air.

For better or worse.

Probably for worse.

Self-defense was, in fact, one thing, as difficult as it was to accept, but actually seeking and destroying enemy aerocraft . . . it didn't seem right, even as I knew it was in the defense of my people, who had taken me and my family in, as well as my squadron mates, with whom I had formed the beginnings of a bond of sorts and they fought for me as I did for them. I really didn't want to hurt anyone anymore, damn it!

And yet, here I was, prepared to begin a career of destruction.

We were all anxiously assembled in the briefing room (newly upholstered mahogany chairs and all, mind you), by means of an emergency meeting one day by the excitable rittmeister, Lothar Schneider. He began drawing pictures on a chalkboard, humming a song to himself. "Some time ago," he said at length, having drawn a picture of a French flier going down, "our forces managed to down a Frog aerocraft, then salvage the wreckage of his crate. Guess what we found?"

The squadron collectively shrugged, unsure.

"These!" he cried triumphantly, making his way over to a nearby table and holding up what appeared to be a pair of propeller blades, each fitted with angled metal brackets. "These pieces face the pilot, so that any bullets fired from his own machine gun that hit the propeller will ricochet off of it, so as not to blow the damn thing away, and yet at such an angle as to not hit the cockpit!" he explained, grunting under the exertion of his load.

"Sounds like quite an advance," I replied grimly. "We should alert all our aerial forces to this development."

"No doubt," said the rittmeister. "He is on to something, Pierrot is! They were clearly researching ways to improve the aim on the machine gun by firing *through* the propeller blades rather than over or around them." He smiled. "Here's the twist. So, it seems, were we!" Grinning, he beckoned us to the hangar. "Come!"

As we followed, we were greeted with the sight of newly uncrated aerocraft—skeletal, single-seater vehicles with one bank of wings, a machine gun, and little more.

The rittmeister continued, "Apparently, some of our scientists have been working on what they call interrupter gear, trying to determine a way for an aeroplane to fire bullets at even timing through the propeller.

The Brits have abandoned their work on it for now. They are, as you know, mounting their propellers at the rear of their fuselages so that the guns have a straight path. These angular brackets, fixed to their propellers, were the best the French did before deciding to mount their guns atop their wings. However," he emphasized with a laugh, "look at what we have in store for the enemy!"

There was some muttering as we inspected the craft. "It doesn't look very stable, sir!" one of the pilots ventured.

"Perhaps not," the rittmeister replied, "but start up the engine and try out the Spandau attached to the machine."

Murmurs of interest arose, and old Heinrich Schmidt, a former infantry officer with a perpetual look of starry-eyed wonder, down to the raised eyebrows and enlarged pupils, took the challenge. Leaping into the cockpit, Schmidt watched the ground crew start his propeller as he engaged the plane's engine; he then took to the sky, firing off a gun salute after he hit a reasonable altitude. "That man is one trusting son of a bitch," one of the other pilots murmured. That said, true enough, at least seventy rounds later, no bullets hit the propeller with nary a jam. The squadron exploded into cheers. I groaned, understanding where this kind of technology would lead us.

"The single-seat Fokker Eindecker I," the rittmeister said dramatically. "I'm looking forward to charting the progress of and competing for aerial victories with you fine gentlemen. Pierrot won't know what hit them!"

It was a very spartan aeroplane, essentially a flying machine gun with wings, but they were ours to marvel at. I decided that it was my hope to claim at least ten aerial victories before the year was out whilst flying these deadly little contraptions.

Deadly, you see, for both pilot and target.

After a quick test flight in which I found the crate's wing-warping controls stiff but adequate, I landed only to learn from the evening papers that a British civilian ocean liner was discovered and boarded by one of our new U-Boats on suspicion of it carrying matériel to France from the United States of America, a country which allegedly touts its neutrality in the face of European politics.

As it should, though the actions of their citizens speak to the contrary.

Sure enough, the ship was found to be secretly conveying supplies, namely machine-gun and rifle ammunition hidden in the decks below the passenger quarters, to the French in Brest. Under duress, the captain of the ship, the so-called *Lusitania*, admitted he was indeed being paid by the French government to use his ship as an easy target, and thus a trap to entice both Britain and America to war if Germans were to sink such a target of opportunity. By preserving the lives of the Americans onboard and letting the British-built *Lusitania* slip by after seizing the magazines bound for France, however, another message was received. The world learned of American smugglers acting separately from their government, and for a time we earned its sympathy, as well as the begrudging thanks of both America and Great Britain for our charity. Hopefully that nefarious plan, having backfired in the Entente's face, might teach them a thing or two about manipulating neutral parties!

5 June 1915

Today, at last, I had a real chance to prove myself useful as an enemy killer and purposeful foiler of their reconnaissance missions. No longer a scout in the air, I have become a duelist! Though I have little experience in enacting the duties of the latter, I hope to learn the art and truly grind to the ground my erstwhile concerns about aviation combat, mostly overcome with my defeat of the DuBois Brothers. There should be no room for fear in the heart of an Imperial German aviator, and, backed by my new comrades, there is no reason for it!

But prior to relating my story of the day, I should like to note that whatever concerns I may have had regarding my worries involving interpersonal relations in this squadron appear unfounded. As with Muller's squadron, FFA 6b is populated by Lutheran squadron mates, save for a single Catholic. Though most of these men are entirely no-nonsense, the eccentric Rittmeister Lothar Schneider promised me from the beginning absolute freedom not just to privately believe in my religion (something, he alleged, that was hurtfully outlawed by our Russian foes) but the freedom to publicly practice such beliefs. "We are a nation of merit," he insisted, and since I had graduated flight school in a time of far less responsive aerocraft, I was to be looked on with respect, no matter my path. To be reminded of this by a believer of this doctrine was a serious relief, and not what I thought would have been the case despite these facts.

Schneider is a lean fellow, quirky and a bookish academic as well. He truly embodies the best parts of the Frankfurt Aviation Society in my past, and looks the part, complete with the dueling scars from his university's fencing salle. He speaks boisterously, is quick to laugh with many a gesture, but is wise nonetheless. He is a formidable pilot who takes his business seriously—he simply thinks he knows how to work a crowd as well.

Alas, his real capacity, for all his brilliance, boisterousness, and general decency, is his wealth. Schneider's father made a killing in the early aerocraft industry working alongside none other than Louis Bleriot and marketing his craft the world over. Such contacts surely must have shoehorned his son, merit or not, to some place of power. And indeed, he did well enough. Alas, he admitted, it was a harsh blow for him, sustained only a few months before, to realize he wasn't nearly as charismatic as he thought, and he admitted he began offering up personal prizes, in addition to encouragement, to keep up squadron productivity.

The fellow I flew alongside in a two-man formation is also not all business, but, alas, in not nearly as accommodating a fashion. Curt Schmidt is a towering, beefy fellow, with fantastic abdominal muscles and a hearty laugh, the latter two of which I wish to compliment him on, but I'm afraid he'd dismiss me as perhaps harboring some manner of attraction to him. Goodness, perhaps I did at first. How grotesque and awkward. Not necessarily because of my attraction, for who am I to judge another, but rather, because once I realized what he laughs about, I noticed the total incompatibility. A dirty joker, he has a thing for filthy magazines and is always out to gather another unscrupulous woman for his harem. All very well—he does what suits him, I do what suits me—except he constantly brags very loudly about his conquests and interrupts conversation on other matters with information to that effect. And oh, yes, he is an anti-Semite—very outspoken about it.

Today we took our birds for another test flight, taking off from our base and zooming along at the breakneck speed of up to 130 kilometers per hour over east-central France! We flew in formation and made a passable team, seeing as Schmidt was the wingleader, myself as the follower, if only because he had been flying with the squadron longer than I and was more insistent about this position.

Much to my relief, the fish were not biting today. We saw two specks in the distance, but as we dove in after them, confident of our ability to fight, we saw on the fuselage of the other machines the symbol of the Iron Cross of Imperial Germany, and realized it was Schneider and his own wingman, fresh from each scoring a kill on their hunt. We turned around and escorted them home, attempting to temper our disappointment in our inability to find quarry of our own.

That was merely day one in my new role as single-seat scout pilot. With both sides bogged down in lines running from Northern France to Switzerland on this front alone, however, with many marches and countermarches, advances and retreats across both sides, the war is fated to drag on, and with it, the infantry will be mired in mud, blood, sweat, and toil, whilst we shall do naught but dip our toes in the various fluids of war.

12 June 1915

A second aerial victory has now been machine-gunned under my belt, this time with my new squadron.

It was not a pretty engagement, but I have learned from it.

Interestingly, having lost my innocence to Giraud and Clouseau, I feel slightly less remorse about the cold-blooded assault I launched upon my foe du jour, an Aéronautique Militaire pilot, one Victor Davide. A regular on my patrol routes when I was an observer with the Sixty-Second FFA, the gentleman had clearly, like myself, changed squadrons to engage in the pleasure and rush of pursuer flight. Strapped into his monoplane Morane-Saulnier Type N, it was interesting to see him in anything but his Caudron with his observer, Jerome, seated behind him. He handled his craft, a former racing plane model, well, but I knew that I would need to knock him from the sky for my own enduring safety's sake. Cleverly maneuvering about the clouds with Curt, my compatriot, at my back, I positioned the sun squarely behind me to reduce visibility of my craft and dove after my quarry, making sure not to go too quickly, lest I shed the delicate wings of my own bird.

I fired, attempting to calculate my gunfire's trajectory whilst factoring in my downwards dive. Bullets spewed from my machine gun at a steady rattle, clearing my propeller and throwing themselves at my foe.

And missed!

The look of disbelief on our faces was a matter of utmost embarrassment as my Fokker screamed past him, shooting ineffectually. He now had the advantage. I attempted to circle around, awaiting my death at any moment, pondering the fact that I had lost my mother's esteem and where I might fall in Hashem's esteem for killing in the name of

Germany, but as my foe came at me, he appeared unable to discharge his Hotchkiss machine gun.

Frustrated, he began pounding at his emplacement. Another jammed gun!

This did not last, however.

Circling around, the two of us jousted each other, Victor's gun now cleared, in our comparable monoplanes, each doing equal and minuscule damage with our short bursts of firepower, so unsteady was our aim. We circled around again, but my machine had the slightest edge in speed and maneuverability, and it was just enough to stabilize and open fire before my foe could tag me first. With a quick burst from Mister Spandau, I snipped off a bit of his wing, further destabilizing the foeman as his French machine began tilting to the right.

He began to run for home as Curt made his attack run, chasing after him until my wingman's engine began to stutter in discontent. In an uncharacteristic act of courtesy, Curt waved me onwards, encouraging me to take the kill shot as he cautiously cut for home. Fortunately, his pursuit of our foe had given me time to line up my attack.

Intent on not letting my quarry go, I chased after Caporal Davide almost single-mindedly, shooting lead into his engine and fuselage. Gouts of smoke began to pour out of his craft as he ducked and juked, attempting to throw off my aim. My coordination allowed me to continue lining up shots that rattled his wings, but he was not about to go down by my hand easily.

Victor went into a nosedive in a final, drastic gesture to avoid further punishment and slip to the safety of his lines. Alas for him, the damage I did was too much for his little machine—his wings snapped and down he tumbled. I could not hear the explosion of the engine from so high above and from over the roar of my engine, but I later buzzed low and saw the ruins of the machine.

Another kill, confirmed or not!

For Fritz.

And yet I still felt a sensation of emptiness. Killing would not bring my gallant friends back.

As I surveyed the grounds, I realized I was on the far side of no-man's-land and had chased my quarry quite a distance. Flying low,

I desperately ducked and weaved amidst the gunshots of the enemy infantry, and had all but made it to safety until:

DAKKADAKKADAKKADAKKA!

Hotchkiss machine-gun fire from anti-aerocraft emplacements amongst the infantry tore into my craft from below, perforating my machine with numerous gaping holes. I kept going, hoping to outrun the range of their attacks as my tail rudder was torn apart by another volley of incoming rounds.

Almost on my side of the trench . . . Just a little bit farther . . .

Safety!

I was then faced with the unenviable task of landing. After some desperate circling, I concluded I had no choice but to crash-land. I managed to find a nice patch of ground to make the attempt, despite the damaged rudder. I lessened the throttle and slowly wrestled the plane toward the ground whilst keeping the nose up. I hit the ground hard and, upon investigation later, found that the wheels had buckled slightly, but I managed to squeal to a stop before I hit a fence protecting a nearby orchard situated next to the aerodrome.

Good enough.

In a small ceremony that followed, I was told that I would have been awarded with the button of a commissioned officer on each side of my uniform's collar and made a leutnant for my commendable conduct—I had survived yet another sortie and brought down an enemy fighter whilst using newly deployed, unorthodox equipment. That was enough for command to take note.

"But," said the rittmeister, with a sorrowful smile, "paperwork for promotions this half has already been submitted and when I tried to enter you in as well, the red tape would not allow it. Strict regimentation rules our empire, you know? Bloody paper pushers!"

He chuckled sadly. "Sorry, Herr Schaefer. Maybe next half year."

Easy for him to say. Once again, they play this Jew for a fool. Infuriating!

Indeed, I realized: I should not be self-conscious and so eager to please my superiors. My flying and combat skills are commendable. They tend to skimp on their encouragements and rewards because I'm Jewish, not because I am undeserving.

My rage simmered somewhat. That was their prerogative.

And their loss.

It was a good day, in its conclusion, for the German Empire, but I found myself harrowed and stressed. I had nearly been killed having performed a series of extremely costly mistakes. And yet, the only way to preserve my existence was to kill, the better to avoid being killed by the Frenchman whom I had struck first. I feel rather dreadful about that. I hope it does not haunt me long, though perhaps it should, as I had conflicted feelings during the fight itself. That should not be the case. I must try to be a man of scruples.

I must maintain what humanity I can in the face of war.

It will be a terribly difficult journey, but I cannot become a monster! I mustn't!

3 July 1915

Today was the day of a most engaging and gut-wrenching endeavor, o Diary. My heart nearly beats its way out of my chest as I write, so terrifying was the encounter, as today I nearly lost my life, saved only by an act of chivalry.

Flying over the French countryside on a lone patrol, I stumbled across an enemy fighter in the distance. A Nieuport 10 model. Roundels, as well as common sense, made him out to be French. Though menacing, as I was somewhat outmatched model for model, I, in my youthful enthusiasm, decided to make him my fourth kill.

To my reckoning, anyway.

Ludwig had to be avenged too.

I had a little bit of fuel left after downing an enemy observation balloon. We jousted one another, testing each other's resolve, before coming about and jousting again. He was brave, I was stupid, and before long his graceful biplane had my relatively clumsy, threadbare monoplane strung out. I was doing my best, but he seemed to be everywhere at once, matching my maneuvers and punishing me with Hotchkiss bullets. Cat and mouse, he chased me a distance over friendly lines, matching me turn for turn in his more maneuverable aerocraft. For all the techniques I learned and put into play both in civilian and military flight school, I could not shake Pierrot today despite my best efforts. I even improvised a few additional tricks that I hoped to remember for later bouts, but to no avail. All of this may well have meant my doom. I held out as long as I could, before, in desperation, I shut off my engine a time to keep from overheating my bullet-riddled machine and attempted to affect a crash landing. This gave me an unusual advantage, as his machine powered past my own. Excited, I took aim and opened fire.

DAKKA—CLICK! DAKKA—CLICK!

Jammed!

Foiled once more, I, frustrated, began furiously pounding my machine gun, hoping to clear the jam. As my foe came around for another pass, I found myself dead in the sky, with only my enemy to grieve my loss.

I would go the way of my past comrades. Fritz . . . Otto . . . Ludwig . . . But no.

As the enemy whipped around me once more, he cut for home, waving jovially as he went. I was in shock. All I recall from then was gaping stupidly as he faded off into the distance. I memorized the name painted onto his craft.

Major Henri DuCoq. It sounded familiar, but in the heat of the moment I could not place the name.

I wondered if I would be as hospitable. Maybe I should consider such a role.

After pondering this thought a moment, I attempted to restart my kite and went into a dive, trying to start my propeller up once more. As my engine began to heat up, protesting with loud squeals and creaks, I found to my great relief that it spluttered and coughed, but roared to life once more, allowing me to land safely behind my lines.

Such a gentleman! I thought I as I flew home. I briefly fancied the thought of becoming a knight in shining armor, only of the skies. But if I was such a soldier, here was a true Siegfried, a Lancelot du Lac! Though I staunched this romantic notion quickly, I could not help but relate the tale to my compatriots, who jested at my good fortune, but I found myself too shocked to join in on the entertaining nature of the evening. Of course, it made sense to conclude that there were some decent Frenchmen, but I never expected to see my life saved by an enemy, much less a French enemy.

But there goes the romanticism again. Mercy does not have to be romantic, and that's all it was, a simple act of mercy. I'm glad it exists, but he should be more careful, in case I was more pragmatic than he expected.

2 August 1915

My Diary,

I have, at long last, made leutnant in the eyes of my fellow pilots. Congratulated with a sizable Sacher torte ordered in from behind our lines, it was a glorious day, to be remembered for some time as I became truly recognized as a great pilot and one amongst my squadron mates, a sentiment I had sorely missed. Hospitality is one thing; belonging is quite another.

Earlier on, my score had stood at four kills, having struck down Davide, Giraud, and Clouseau, another enemy flier, as well as an observation balloon, since my debacle with that gallant knight, DuCoq. Certainly not a poor score, but I was determined to improve my pace. After many adventures, having narrowly evaded death several times in months past, I had become cautious, retreating at the first sign of serious danger. Though I understood someone still had to attempt to shoot enemy birds from the sky and it fell to me to do so, I also knew that Germany was financially outmatched and suffered heavy losses at the hands of the suddenly superior planes flown by our foes. Cowed by this line of thought, day after day I tried to find individual enemies I might ambush from the clouds on my patrols. But the Entente, in turn, had grown leery of our so-called "Fokker Scourge," a wild belief that *their* excessive losses were due to an alleged fleet of our Eindeckers and their synchronized machine guns (we actually only had about fifty total), rather than their pilots' own stupidity. They, as well, had begun to fall back at the very sight of us.

It had become extremely exasperating.

About a week and a half after I came to this conclusion—ten whole days of the enemy avoiding me—I, in my utmost desperation and spoiling for some action, sought out a more stationary, but no less challenging, target—another observation balloon—during one of my routine patrols in friendly territory as I crossed over our infantry dugouts.

Whilst not an actual aeroplane, such a target nonetheless counts as a kill upon its undoing. The loss of a balloon is heavily celebrated by the victorious party, you see, for its extreme usefulness to its owners.

There did it float, an enormous, bloated bag of hot air, its crew directing artillery through a wireless device. Normally I would feel a little guilty about taking down an unarmed observation craft. Memories of the DuBois brothers flickered in my mind, but I quenched them quickly. The balloon was responsible for all manner of hell upon our poor infantry and had to be stopped!

Climbing rapidly amidst the clouds of flak from the anti-aerocraft batteries defending the balloon that rained around me as I crossed over into enemy lines, watching apprehensively as shrapnel bounced off my craft, I managed to position myself above the cumbersome gasbag, making it harder for enemy fire to hit me. Coming about and diving sharply downwards as flak barrages blasted around me, making me wince, I let loose with Mister Spandau and poked the balloon full of many small holes. At length, clouds began pouring from each of the balloon's many gaping pores. It flopped gracelessly to the ground in a heap as I gradually pulled out of my dive.

Unfortunately, with the behemoth defeated, the anti-aerocraft gunfire was at last able to draw a more accurate bead on me and the world around me exploded. Engulfed in a cloud of flak as I pulled up, I could feel my craft being torn apart by small metal shards. I roared in exertion as the splinters whizzed by my face, and punched the throttle of my aeroplane, mercifully pushing through the attack and emerging with my craft in working condition, albeit on its last legs and rent full of holes. Pushing my Fokker to its limits whilst yanking hard on the control stick and ruddering hard to the right, I attempted to make a break for home, doing everything I could to evade a second volley and climb, climb, climb! My plane jumped as though stung by a wasp and surged homeward. Alas, it resented my rough treatment and squealed angrily in response to my violent methods. Realizing that I would be ill-advised to snap off components of my craft, I lessened my grip on the plane and came about more gradually.

Shells exploded around me as I wrestled for control of my plane, but at last, I prevailed, speeding for home, dodging lead almost every step of the way over no-man's-land before making it to friendly lines.

I was safe, if only for the day, but an ace at long last.

My euphoria was surely palpable, and my squadron mates, quick to decipher my facial expression, were delighted to celebrate the affair with me. A party was soon thrown for me forthwith. Women were summoned, as were wine and song, and a joyous time was had by all. Whether or not I had the best of times in the company of these revelers was up to question, but I was happy to see my friends have a glad time in my name.

As I enjoyed the company and endured numerous jocular toasts, I could hear the roar of engines overhead as the latest flight patrol returned home late with two men missing. When I learned that the French pilot DuCoq was responsible, my mind began to race.

This was the same pilot who spared me.

DuCoq . . . Mein Gott! This was the pilot whom I had met in my younger years! The fellow I had alienated when he had helped me through flight school!

I must seek him out again.

For what purpose? I am unsure.

30 August 1915

Today, injured, I dictate this piece, rather than write it by hand. I should like to thank my childhood friend, Christianne, who serves as one of my tender nurses, for her assistance in transcribing this work.

Ahem.

I awoke this day to find myself hospitalized and under the care of a gaggle of nurses in a hospital some forty-eight kilometers behind Bühl. It is a dark, dank place, and I could only make out so much of it through the bloodstained curtains which obscured my vision and insight into the rest of the place, shielding me, one might say, from the horrors within. Surrounded by the injured, with the moans of the wounded regularly punctuated by the sharp, sudden, prolonged cries of the newly amputated, this new environment came as a shock to me, if only a slight one. For last I was awake, I had been frantically dodging anti-aerocraft fire and returning it with gusto, to help our bombers support an impending assault on Pierrot's lines.

From the beginning, I had thought it an inauspicious day. The clouds threatened, and heavy winds again buffeted my craft. I recollected this weather from my fight against the Russians on the Eastern Front, and I thought it very likely our beloved rittmeister would cancel the patrol in the first place on account of the bad weather, but high command would not have it. Thus, we persisted, and sallied despite the complications.

Flying high over little French villages occupied by our men, made positively tiny by the height of two thousand meters at which I flew, I attempted to avoid detection for as long as I could. At length, I saw the trenches of no-man's-land cutting deep into the dirt as I wondered how many soldiers would die on both sides attempting to take a few meters of soil. My mind crossed over to considering the unusual, but also the horrific—how many not just humans but animals, above ground and subterranean, would lose their homes to this vicious fighting, for example. Too many, I was sure.

War makes monsters of us all.

Upon spotting my target, a regiment of Frogs in their trenches below, I swooped in to deliver my payload of lead. Casings flew freely as I pinned down the enemy forces, leaving a trail of dead bodies in my wake. In doing so, I thought myself a coward, attacking all but defenseless foes on the ground, but then I realized that in addition to being a duelist, I was a defender, protecting my charges, the German infantry, as they advanced and took the position held by French infantry. Therefore, it was reasonable to come about for another pass, intent on working over the Frog machine-gun nests, oiled and readied, prepared to cut down my men by the thousands. As I sallied forth, I could see our brave lads emerge from the trenches and rush the enemy, surely with a cry all but unheard to me under the roar of my engine.

Whipping my bird about, I blasted away at the enemy nests, both anti-aerocraft and anti-infantry machine guns in variety. They were protected by sandbags but still somewhat exposed to enemy fire from above. Someone needed to protect our poor bloody infantry, and that somebody was me. Flying a route roughly parallel to the trenchlines, I successfully de-crewed several enemy guns, but the infantry, slowly rallying, began firing at my aeroplane. At length, a lucky shot tore into my engine, which began to leak, bleeding away my plane's life profusely. I decreased the throttle to avoid heating my leaking fuel supply too much and attempted to glide away, but it was too late.

Cracklecracklecrackle WHOOOOOOOOOOOOSH!

The plane had caught flame!

I do not believe I need tell you, dear Diary, how dire the straits of an individual are when they are caught in a flaming machine of canvas and wood. I immediately dove toward no-man's-land, thinking it better to take my chances there than in a burning plane, and, flames licking at my hindquarters, leapt from the cockpit about two meters, and tumbled to my fate out of the craft. My skull scarcely missed an outcropping of rocks, as the plane promptly flipped over and exploded nearby.

All then went black.

According to the German Greycoat troops who found me, I had been rescued as they secured the French trenches. It all seemed reminiscent of my crash that had resulted in Otto's death, and I wept, thinking about it. Brought back to our lines by a stretcher, I was grouped alongside grievously wounded ground troops and rushed to a hospital. Now as I wake, surrounded as I am by grief and depression, I wish to God I would have died in the inferno.

Though Christianne herself, much to my surprise, numbers amongst the nurses at the encampment, and it is more wonderful than ever to see her alive and well as we joke and smile and reminisce about the old days, but the pain we both feel is incalculable. I can tell she remains tremendously melancholy after her brother's death and made more so by her job and its emotional and physical difficulties, and the trauma I feel is also difficult to surmount. A part of me wishes to escape the war and evade all the death and killing by merit of my wounds—the most major of which is a wrist fractured by the crash, as well as a few burns—but that would be dishonorable and, worse, a disservice to my family and people. It would also not be enough.

Closing my eyes for a feverish nap after a meager repast, positively spartan compared to the food at the aerodrome, I regard the field soldiers with pity, having been relegated to mediocre rations, stuck in trenches, and rattled by disease and enemy fire for the duration of the war so far. At least the war is over for these poor sods, hospitalized by their injuries, as they are. It can only get worse for the others.

I am going to rest myself for now. Perhaps when I awaken this nightmare will be over.

20 September 1915

My beloved Diary,

After many days of physical therapy and great pain, I have regained my ability to write, if only a little bit now and then, and will cautiously continue to do so from here on out.

Still in the hospital, I have at last been permitted to lurk about with a hand in a brace. I have visited my fellows in the hospital, including a gentleman I knew from the Sixty-Second FFA, recently transferred to this front. A flier, wounded in the head, by the name of Oswald Boelcke, he was cold company, only intent on writing a book of tactics for aviation combat, and I quickly grew disinterested in his indifferent, calculating manner. It was lonely to be left to my devices, but he was bereft of charm in body, mind, and soul regardless. What's more, he was only there for a few days, only had a minor wound, and transferred out in due time. I am jealous of his good fortune. I must return to my base, to my friends, and maybe, to seek out DuCoq!

Whether to avenge my brother fliegers or to reunite with an old friend, I know not.

I continue to have my share of difficulty and at this time hope I am not discharged from service for the injuries I have sustained. I wonder if I can still fly with my once-injured wrist, for whilst it is on the road to recovery, what twists and turns of fate lie ahead? As I wait for my answer, I note that I can take this opportunity to keep good company with the artillerists, infantrymen, and cavalry troopers injured at the front. According to one of the cavalrymen, recently transferred to the front from the Russian war and being fitted for a prosthetic arm, he knew of dear Ludwig, and had kind words to say of our handsome, burly war hero. Alas, it did not ease my emotional scars—as for my physical ones, my left wrist can flex and bend, but this brings about great pain. Progress is slow and disheartening.

Worsening the situation, the artillerists and infantry look upon me with a bit of scorn and seem to attempt to keep to a protective clique of their own as I attempt to interact with them. Each clique's responses in conversation are laconic and gruff, as they turn their backs on me in as polite a way as possible. Perhaps they are sullen about the airs of aristocracy many pilots affect. I understand some see issue with these mannerisms and I surely did not mean to exert any superiority over the ground forces myself, but the conversation I attempted to start up with Mister Boelcke did not help matters, as we must have seemed elitist in front of the line men thanks to the monied background from which we hail. I tried to apologize, was told to think nothing of it, and still have been snubbed. So it goes. At least the cavalry is a bit more understanding, tending to come from money themselves. Using my background and time with Ludwig, I'm able to keep up a running conversation with his brethren and can wow them with stories of my endeavors, though I'm sure they also do not like what might be seen as bragging about my illustrious career. One trooper catches my eye as a patient, benevolent individual—worthy of my time and once a strong soldier and horseman before his injury, a fractured knee. Unfortunately, his status as a cavalryman and build as such reminded me closely of my handsome and brave Ludwig. I would be consistently reminded of his gallantry in this young man and that would depress me. As such, I could not approach him, for all his ready smiles and melodious laughter. I never even asked him his name.

Christianne, however, has been good company throughout my tribulations. Over the course of my tenure here, she has smuggled me cigarettes and cake. She has also taken me out for walks. As we exercise my wrist together, she is congratulatory and very sweet as I make progress and supportive even if I regress. We lift weights, and she hugs me and nurtures me with each dumbbell I graduate to. We continue to speak of the old days, but I can also tell that she wants to press the topic of romance as well, offering to be my wife. I find this most unprofessional, considering the status of our nurse-patient relationship, and am unsure how to take this matter onto my shoulders. To stall her, I told her that I loved her, for my life was in her hands, and because I do, in fact, care deeply for her as a friend, but continued to say that I was unsure if during war was the best time to raise a family, especially of two warriors. She conceded the fact but would not drop the line of discussion.

The poor dear.

The foolish, vile me.

For I could not bring myself to tell her I could never love her in that way. After much thought allowable only when one is indisposed, I came to the conclusion that I not only preferred the company of gentlemen, I had no romantic interest in women at all. Could I, perhaps, find some forbidden joy in men?

Ahem . . .

Well, I must recover. This is certainly not something to think on right now.

10 October 1915

At long last, I have been discharged from the hospital.

My body has not sustained any lasting injuries.

My only wish is that I could have served my countrymen better during my absence. I feel as though I have failed my fellow pilots and soldiers.

Deep down, I know I have done my best so far, but the feeling of inadequacy, that I was downed by enemy fire—infantry fire, no less (though perhaps I should not be so derogatory of our fellows on the ground)—and that I lay inert upon a bed for over a month or so, feels so terribly disheartening. All these fine gentlemen, doing their best to defeat the French, whilst I could do naught but look on.

In the end, Christianne drove me home (if home would be my aerodrome), and reintroduced me to the squadron. Though this was welcome news, it was not, to me, cause for celebration. As her motor car conveyed me back to the base, she discussed our future together at some length. After about an hour of her diatribes and my noncommittal grunts, I could take it no more. "Christianne," said I, taking her hand in my own, "I do not wish you any harm by saying so, but much as I love you as I would a sister, and always will, you must understand that I see you as more a friend or sibling than a wife. You have been loyal and true, but I cannot help but admit that, in honesty, I prefer the company of men. I hope you understand and accept this about me."

Christianne's look of shocked disappointment rent my heart in twain, sullying the day's celebrations all the more. As I pecked her on the cheek with great care, but clearly not with the emotion she wanted, she burst into tears, ceasing only as I hugged her tight.

Meanwhile, back at the aerodrome, I was saluted, wined, and dined by my fellows, who clearly wanted to make a considerable affair of my return. I was quick to raise my hand and halt any further revelry. "No gentlemen," said I. "It is more important to celebrate the land gained in today's push against the enemy." This silenced them a moment before young, idealistic Lothar Schultz, a recruit when I first was hospitalized, now a pilot with two kills under his belt but as innocent a look as ever, spoke up.

"Why not both?"

My mood lifted a bit at this as I favored Lothar with a tentative smile, which was responded to with a broad, if tragically homely, smile of his own.

Many lost teeth and blackened lips, you see . . .

I then remembered that he had been an athlete in years past, a famous footballer who quit to serve his country.

I was glad, however, that the fellows actually seemed to care some-what about me. Arm in arm, we traipsed about the streets of war-torn Germany, such that a passerby might deem us delirious with war wea-riness. They did, at the very least, shut themselves indoors as we passed.

Tomorrow we would once more spill blood, soldiers yet again, but tonight we would carouse!

We crashed loudly into a café with a small collection of civilians milling about, and we ordered some of their best brandy and drank lib-erally to the accompaniment of cheese and sausage. I again dispensed with my Jewish tradition, the better to enjoy the latter delicacy. This done, we played many cards and billiards games and talked the evening away. I was told that we currently enjoy significant superiority in the air over the Entente, and that our machines are a runaway success over that of our enemy's. We shall see if this lasts, but even if it does not, we apparently have numerous new models under development to push our advantage.

This was all very well, I noted, but whether the Entente had refined their tactics last I had taken to the skies, was a question worthy of wonder.

It turns out I had nothing to worry about. And even if I did, with my comrades at my back, I felt somewhat secure.

30 October 1915

Today, in the form of a startling announcement, we received word of some exciting news. Firstly, that the fellow who had started this war on a more superficial level (as I now believe, after some discussion with my comrades, that conflict was sure to have broken out eventually), Gavrilo Princip, has been sentenced to twenty years in prison. Not nearly enough, I would say, for having caused such havoc and cruelty already, but he was under twenty years of age, so they let him off easy. Disappointing, but we forgot all about this letdown in the face of surprise reinforcements. They were furry, four-legged, and absolutely adorable. In brief, Brunhilde, our beloved squadron mascot, mostly Doberman with some slight shepherd blood in her, gave birth to a litter of pups. This has raised FFA 6b's morale, as we celebrated the new recruits with a rousing cheer and a toast. "Such energy and loyalty as these dogs are sure to present to their masters will be rewarded," the rittmeister declared very formally, attempting to look serious despite cuddling one of the puppies as the mother looked on. "Let us hope our mouser cat tolerates their existence!"

Then, much to my intense jealousy, the ground crew was promptly called upon to look after the puppies and the new mother, making all essential preparations to see to their comfort. *I could have done that just as well!* I thought, having pored over so many dog-rearing manuals. The pups were to be the property of the FFA 6b at large, the rittmeister decided, but as the ground crew were ever so much handier, surely they could learn to take care of the hounds too, as we pilots were otherwise occupied with our flying. I was unsure how being handy with hardware made the ground crew any more capable of caring for the puppies and remain pretty sure the rittmeister merely wanted him and his charges to be saddled with as few duties as possible, but I was grateful the dogs would have a good home, even if I could not practice the dog-rearing that I had studied so intently as a youth. Nonetheless, I could at least now see why we pilots were thought upon as snobs. With staffs of cooks, engineers, and batmen dogging, or perhaps, hounding our every step, we were rather well-endowed with aid many only needed because they were generally raised with noble blood.

10 November 1915

Good Sir Diary,

The French fliers released several bombs onto the airfields of one of our sister squadrons. To their credit, their observers sighted for the bombs very well and the ordnance flew with marked accuracy into a hangar and a barracks, as well as burst atop two of our fellows' grounded Fokker E.Is.

In my efforts to make up for the fact that I have been in the hospital the past few months, I may have tried too hard this day. Having met a friend whilst flying over our lines in what was to become an offensive patrol, it nearly led to my undoing.

This other fellow flew an elderly design, a Caudron, to be exact.

More Frogs.

Upon seeing me, they took off, seeking to reach friendly lines before I shot them from the skies. He and his gunner led me on a merry chase. Unfortunately for them, my height permitted me to dive after them, picking up even more speed when I already had this advantage, as I dove downwards to close the gap between our two machines.

As we bobbed and weaved across no-man's-land, by no means silent at this time in its own right, as a Frog attack was underway beneath us, I realized, almost too late, that I had focused all my energy in striking down that machine from the sky. Looking around, I found we had crossed deep into enemy territory. Still intent on bringing my foe down, I danced with the observer plane, attracting the attention of French scouts. I noticed the newcomers to be elegant machines, those damnable Nieuport 10s, which individually already posed a considerable match to my aeroplane: my Eindecker was slower and less maneuverable. It was only better as a gun platform, in which sense I could fire straight across, and through the propeller, rather than over it at an angle.

Taking notice of the planes' markings, I noticed that the Caudron had led me back to the Escadrille N73's aerodrome. These fellows were known to be a band of gentlemen pilots with a tendency for flight excellence. And now, two of them had begun to chase me, with two more taking to the skies to join in the fun.

I was now compelled to turn tail and run, though before I did, I snapped off several rounds from my machine gun at the launching craft, disrupting one plane's takeoff as it turned sharply to avoid both being struck and nearly crashing to the ground. Not about to revel in my victory just yet, I yelped as my crate was shredded up by the previously hunted Caudron pilot, now the hunter.

Turning for home, followed by my pursuers, I streaked toward no-man's-land, pushing our machines to their limits. Unfortunately, a second, precise volley fired by a Nieuport hit my engine. Amidst the sputtering and smoking, I was forced to slow down to avoid further strain, delicate as my craft was. Not one to surrender to my enemies at the first bit of damage done to my craft, however, I turned to fight, expecting to die. Juking and bobbing wildly, we passed each other twice, whilst the other foemen followed close behind, trying to get a clean shot. All hope was not lost, however. Two angels from friendly squadrons, the Iron Cross of Germany painted on their fuselages, had flown onto the scene, and joined me in taking on my foes in a general engagement. I waved to them my thanks as they passed me by, before firing on a Nieuport pilot who responded in kind.

As the battle raged about one hundred meters above me, evolving toward the front, I realized I was not of much assistance to my allies. Terrifyingly enough, my original prey, the Caudron, again sought to bring me down, screaming down upon me from above, machine gun blazing. I dodged the blasts to the best of my ability, but my single, enormous bank of wings were difficult targets to miss. Indeed, his plane was a potentially formidable foe when attacked from the front, and with my rear to its front, I was in a perilous position.

Banking hard to the right as the Caudron's gunfire strafed my wings, I fell toward the tree line on their side of the trenches, pulled up harshly at the last second, and just managed to avoid scraping the belly of my beast along the birches below. At this point, I attempted to limp back to friendly lines, undetected.

I was not so lucky.

RATATATATATA!

The French observer opened up on me from his gun mount, striking my engine once more, which went up in flames.

Scheiße.

I immediately shut down my engine, which slowed the flow of flames, and attempted a crash landing. I cringed at the gut-wrenching KRACHT as my poor Fokker touched down, her landing gear crushed as she swerved around in a circle. Barely wasting a second to grab you, o Diary, I leapt from my vehicle and evacuated my craft.

It exploded with a resounding BOOM!

I apologize for singeing your pages, Diary, as I now regard my surroundings. I am alone and frightened, and feel all but assured of my capture. Having already been injured for some portion of the conflict, I feel remorseful. I may be sitting out the rest of the war now, thanks to my single-minded enthusiasm. Curse my impulsive nature! Curse the French!

My heart ached for Ludwig. Christianne. Fritz. Otto.

Anyone?

No one.

Curse this war.

10 November 1915

Dear Diary,

I write from captivity now, a prisoner of Escadrille N73. As my plane was destroyed in pitched combat earlier today, I had had enough of fighting for one afternoon. Knowing the French infantry would likely shoot me as a downed enemy pilot, jealous of the luxury in which I live and wracked by the actions of my people during the 1870 war, I therefore sought out the hospitality of their pilots. With trenchlines full of French troops in pitched combat against my Greycoats, dashing my every effort to get home, my only hope lay in their pilots treating a fellow knight of the air and man of means as an equal!

Taking to the trees to duck past approaching patrols, even as I knew most of the enemy French troops were on the attack at this time, I wrapped my fur coat close around me, Luger tucked inside, but at the ready, I made my way toward the N73's aerodrome.

As I approached, a tall, rail-thin fellow and his shorter, stout compatriot stepped out from inside their barracks. Leisurely striding over to a nearby motor car, the tall one elected to ignore the open passenger door and instead sat in the driver's position, politely gesturing to his batman to step out and take the passenger's seat. The two zoomed off in my direction, and, as it neared, I perceived the vehicle to be a jaunty brick red in hue and built along beautiful lines over which Ludwig himself would drool. The two crept to a stop as they exited and made their way up to me, hands on the holsters of their revolvers. "Greetings, flieger," the tall fellow said gently in my language, as I suddenly became aware of a small squad of French troops coming up behind him, rifles at the ready. He extended his hand for my Luger with all the chivalry of a knight of centuries past. "Come! There are wolves and, worse," he gestured to the soldiers, "infantrymen crawling in these woods." He laughed airily. "Allow us to offer you hospitality a time. We will ensure your squadron mates and family will be notified that you are a prisoner, and not deceased, and will treat you with all the gentility we can a captive." He clapped his hand upon his automobile. "Here. Join us in my motor car! My name is DuCoq, by the way."

He smiled and even thanked me as he gently confiscated my Luger, but what enraptured me was his name.

DuCoq!

It is him, I thought. *The fellow who spared my life in aerial combat not long ago!* He looked familiar enough—as dashing and genteel as I thought he would be: tall and possessed of a pencil mustache as thin as his physique. His comrade was nothing to look at, but I was likely too taken with my discovery to notice him anyway. I blushed and turned away, but couldn't help but be drawn back to gaze at his statuesque features.

Despite my less than hygienic state, with sweat and burns and oil stains all over my vestments, the major gallantly offered me a seat in his vehicle. I found myself lost in his blue eyes and blond hair and nodded stupidly, before seating myself in the passenger seat. This left the batman to walk. He seemed used to it.

Back at the French aerodrome, a spacious, if not altogether welcoming locale, endowed with many anti-aerocraft guns, a small garrison force of infantry, a stockade, farm, and motor pool. As DuCoq parked his vehicle here, I noticed it comprised many staff cars, each smelling heavily of gasoline and oil, having been newly serviced. It was a very homey, pleasant tang.

I was given the full hospitality by my foes, as though I were an honored guest. All manner of exotic British teas, French cheeses, and Belgian chocolates found their way down my gullet, as I laughed and joked in German with my captors, who, almost to a man, kindly obliged to use my own language. There was much to chuckle about, especially so when we shared stories of how our interests in flight first came into being. When I spoke of my accidental encounter alongside my beloved Ludwig, making mention as to the reckless acrobatic pilot, DuCoq's jaw dropped. "That was me!" he exclaimed. HA! So it was!

So, we pilots cynically and hopelessly toasted (in my opinion rather tastelessly, as men were dying) to our frustration at Russian (in their case), as well as Austro-Hungarian (from my perspective) incompetence. "Long may they balance each other out," DuCoq remarked sarcastically, "that we might fight out this oh so lovely war forever."

We also toasted to poor plane design, and we even touched upon history and changing politics over years past. One of the Frenchmen then played lively music on a piano as the rest of us danced to the upbeat tune. We all shared stories of our lives and times and I ruefully discussed with DuCoq how things proceeded after flight school and why I stopped writing to him. If DuCoq was upset, he did not show it, but his concern appeared palpable. "I assumed you went on to newer and better things," he replied. "I wish I had known exactly how bad it was for you, but I assumed you came upon a stroke of good fortune that caused you to stop needing to write! That you had begun to belong! Oh Max . . . I am so sorry! I do hope they treat you better now during the war proper?"

And so I told them of my complications. How my subordinates would salute me, but gossip behind my back, how my superiors would pass me over for promotion. "It is a nightmare," I said, "But one I must learn to suffer through like everyone else."

DuCoq's wingmen, despite seeming to sympathize with me along with their master, knew their duties well. In their merriment, they began to sweetly and jovially ask about my knowledge of positions and tactics, attempting to work them into casual conversation and take advantage of my inebriation from the party. Their attempts were underhanded and feeble—I was too wise for these interrogation tactics.

Or so I recall, as the French wines had taken a toll on my senses.

However manipulative, these Frenchmen were just doing their job, though, trying to make the best of a bad situation, and were not so terrible once you got a chance to know them.

Even as they hoped to conquer us.

Had it been but a hundred years ago, I may not have held this against them. To this day, I do not either. We were made to understand as youths in school that back then that their empire was singly the strongest and most cultured, after all. Now, however, despite an ailing Kaiser, we are told that Germany has a culture, military, and intellect unlike and far and above any other in the world. That there are many Frenchmen, Englishmen, and indeed, people the world over, who would kill for such educations, such military training, and such access to exciting opportunities.

Bollocks, I now thought. *The French and English are a proud people with strong traditions and backgrounds to marvel at as well. If not, I* asked the propagandist in my head, *wouldn't they permit us to spread the word of our achievements and attributes, instead of fight us? We would be sure to best them in combat, so why would they attack us so?*

As the French pilots jested about my culture's militant, disciplined history, and that yet they managed to claim me as a captive, I nearly told them jokingly in return about my education on French culture from the German perspective—that they were cowardly and frivolous and ate the most ridiculous cuisine, but bit my tongue for fear of offending others with my "learnings," even if it would have been meant facetiously and that I would have started with that. I was also already their prisoner and did not need to be brutalized by their enraged, vengeful hand should they take my remarks the wrong way.

As I turned in for the night in the French stockade, having been gently escorted at DuCoq's reluctant orders by the MPs local to the French aerodrome, I found the conditions far less friendly than the lounge in which I gamboled with the "friendly" enemy pilots. As rats scrambled amidst the wooden planks making up the floor, I found few comforts save a warped cot and a moth-eaten blanket to sleep with. A rusty sink and privy rounded out the accommodations.

As I was curling up in my questionable conditions, I heard a lightly knock sound on my door and the curt words "Tu es relevé" spoken to some individual or another outside my door, presumably my guards. The door opened to reveal DuCoq! He came with a dressing gown for me and was accoutered in his uniform, but upon entering and closing the door, promptly stripped down to a nightgown of his own. I couldn't help but gawk at how beautifully his gown fit his perfectly toned body, feeling a combination of admiration, slight envy, and, I shan't deny it, a degree of lust as I feasted my eyes upon him. Here was a man who seemed to care for me, who was there for me, and was more than just a pretty face. His soothing, calm voice, his steady gaze, the adorable way he steepled his fingers as he spoke . . .

For a moment I wished I could join him in his bed, rather than rest upon the cot procured for me. He seemed entirely unbothered by this.

"Take all the time you desire, flieger," he remarked with a teasing smile. "The guards have gone. I have volunteered to watch you myself. And clearly you, me. Though I might suggest that it is refreshing to sleep in the nude. Join me, if you dare," he winked coquettishly.

Who was I to back down from a challenge?

27 November 1915

Dear Diary,

It appears chivalry is alive and well amongst the Frogs, even if both our armies are encouraging the men to avoid such displays of gallantry. "This is a war!" those in Berlin, Paris, Moscow, Vienna, Rome, Istanbul, and Sofia announce. "Even the aviators must take a role!" they cry. "Yes!" the aviator replies grimly, a flicker of a smile across his face. "But when you strike someone from the sky, politeness costs nothing, and reaps a great reward."

The honor of the N73s has soared above and beyond the call of duty today, dear Diary. In accordance with their high command, who proclaimed me a prisoner of war, they kept me in their custody, yes, but treated me almost as one of their own, short of briefly confiscating you, issuing a curfew, and only letting me wander certain regions of their base, whilst under guard.

Fair enough.

The Frogs did me a damn fine turn, for as they wined and dined me, they also drove me back to the trenches and ordered an infantry detail to return me to my lines in exchange for a pilot of their own captured earlier in the day, elsewhere in the front. "Never forget, sir, that you are a Prussian eagle," DuCoq explained to me fondly. "Eagles deserve better than to be caged. So far as I see it? You will die with dignity, or you will live through this war." He patted me on the shoulder and smiled. It was a fond tap, and his smile sent a pleasant shiver down my spine. His teeth were straight and white like a military cemetery.

As I emerged from the vehicle and two surly-looking soldiers roughly grabbed hold of me, I called after DuCoq, "Will I ever see you again?"

His reply was to point grimly to the darkened skies. "As feuding angels in the skies above."

"Foes though we may be, let us be friendly foes!" I replied as the low-born men of Marseille in their horizon-blue uniforms began to lead me off. "May we be sportsmen, not assassins!"

"So may it be," DuCoq replied. He ran after us and upon catching up with the Marseille soldiery took them by the shoulder and spoke to them in a rapid fusillade of French.

I admired deeply the good major's knowledge of a plethora of dialects and languages, along with his ability to mingle with those beneath him, as well.

Under a white flag of truce, Pierrot reintroduced me to my allies, and thankfully, though perhaps because they did not seem to think highly of the airmen, the infantry on our side believed my tale. They were not amused, however, as they seemed to understand war to be a far more serious matter in the trenches below.

Begrudgingly, with much muttering amongst themselves, the regiment of Bavarian soldiers who received me loaded me into a lorry and drove me back to the aerodrome. As though afraid to touch me, assuming my higher rank in society, being a pilot, they merely gestured me from the machine and walked me to the rittmeister's office. It was good to be home, but everyone looked at me as though I hailed from another planet altogether. Schneider looked me up and down as I told my story, as though not believing me, yet recognizing it to be me. "But *why* would they let you go, Schaefer?" he kept asking, myself responding time and time again that it was an unusual matter of trading prisoners, until at length, my compatriots, hearing the ruckus, rushed into the officer's quarters to welcome their lost brother home. At length, Schneider sighed. "Welcome back. Rest well. We have much to discuss tomorrow."

As I reveled with my fellows once more, however, I now felt a tad morose to return to my aerodrome. Though Germany has a wonderful culture and education system, it certainly does not show in the trenches, and, for one curious moment, I missed imprisonment already. No more killing? Luxurious treatment? It was quite a bit of indulgence, considering our time in history.

28 November 1915

Diary, a coup has been struck against my emotional well-being. A logical one, of course, as the Fatherland, whilst occasionally subconsciously hurtful, would likely not knowingly steer me wrong, but it will be a sadness to not be able to see my French friends again.

Over breakfast today, Rittmeister Schneider and I met. Dog on his lap, after offering me one to balance precariously upon my own (I accepted with glee), he loosened my lips with brandy, and we talked as friends about my meeting with the N73s. After delighting in hearing about my grounding of an enemy fighter in the conflict leading up to my meeting DuCoq, he of course showed concern for my personal well-being when I got to the part when I was shot down, kindly ordering bedrest for me yet another day, but also betrayed great distress about the kind treatment the French gave me, and frequently inquired after whether or not I'd be capable of continuing to fly against them and be willing to knock them from the sky. I assured him my loyalty to the Fatherland was stronger than a few signs of goodwill, and this seemed to satisfy him, but did not keep him from reminding me that the goodwill was likely a show, likely so that they might better undermine my feelings of hostility.

I am not sure I believe this, however. The rittmeister, though respectable and wise, and probably right regarding some Frenchmen, perhaps many, is wrong about Major DuCoq. He is a man to be respected, and though I obviously will not risk being shot down again to spend time with him, I will not go out of my way to slay him. As I parted company with the rittmeister, I could not help but feel that if I had ever possessed strong, positive feelings about entering this war, I no longer did. I lay back upon my bunk, mercifully more comfortable than the one I had whilst a prisoner of the French, and meditated upon the fact that the loss of many clearly respectable individuals from amongst the soldiers of all nations is grievous, and that even still, we pilots, wrongfully indoctrinated to be and seemingly valued above them in social rank as we frequently are, do not know the whole of it in the least. Pilot, soldier, or sailor, the flowers of so many nations, are dying like flies, and at this rate, there will be few accomplished enough to run this nation. Still, this is a war of the self-preservation of the only recently cobbled together Empire of Germany. Austria-Hungary and Turkey are doomed to falter and recede in territory, and I shall not miss either in their past forms, but Germany? Germany, you have only just come into being and hold such promise. Must you fall to the might and tyranny of the Entente? Will the reduction or destruction of our state by the perfidy of the French government, the greed of the Italian King and parliament, or the bloodlust of the Russian Czar truly be our fate?

Fortunately, we continue to do well against the Russians, from what I read, and whilst the sick men of Europe, such as Austria-Hungary, who continues to crumble, and our other major ally, the Ottoman Turks, who lose ground too, we shall honor these alliances we have made. Even if we fall, our nation of warriors will be defeated with smiles of grim determination upon our faces.

My ruminations were disturbed by the return of the lads from a football match. Judging by the state of their clothes and the smiles upon their sweat-stained faces, it must have been an intense and even affair. I partook in their shenanigans once they had undressed, showered, and shaved, playfully tussling with them before bedtime was called. *It was good to be back amongst my fellows*, I thought. I should have watched their match and bonded with them.

The Schaefer family
leaves Vienna for
Germany. 1879.

Maxwell and his
childhood friends
Ludwig and
Christianne Becker
frolic on horseback.
1913.

A young Schaefer, Ludwig, and Christianne partake in a jolly picnic in the German countryside. 1913.

A student of the Frankfurt Aviation Society, Schaefer thoughtfully examines his Bleriot training craft from afar. 1913.

Schaefer and Otto, his observer, proudly displaying their most recent photograph. 1914.

Schaefer and his squadron mates marvel at a newly unboxed Fokker Eindecker I. 1915.

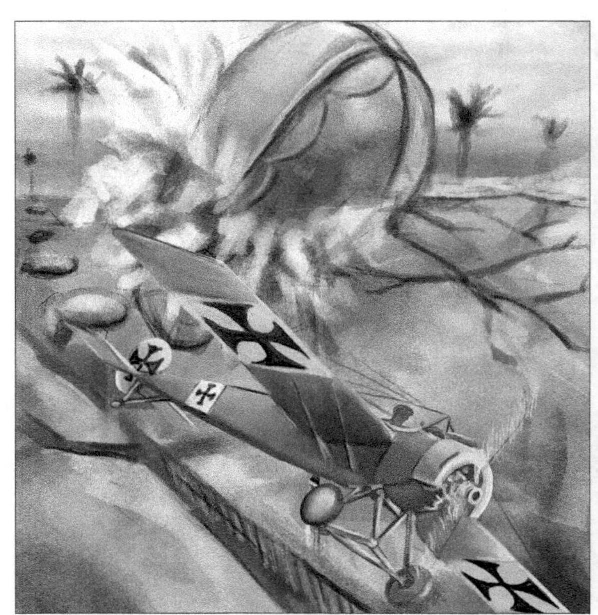

With a resounding
explosion, Schaefer
destroys an enemy
observation balloon.
1915.

Major Henri DuCoq
of L'Aeronautique
Militaire. 1915.

Schaefer alongside some fellow pilots of the FFA 6B. 1916.

Schaefer, heavily engaged with a Nieuport 11 of the Lafayette Escadrille. 1916.

Maxwell Schaefer and family. 1916.

Schaefer and his Ottoman allies enjoying a repast in Palestine. 1918.

30 November 1915

Diary, today was quite the experience to say the least, and I am glad to have survived, shaken though I am. Whilst feasting upon some bratwurst earlier this evening after a fruitless patrol, with the sky as dense as pea soup, I happened upon the notion that I wished to learn how to assist the ground crews in tending to my craft, for what good is a pilot without a mechanic if no such skills were possessed? In a recent sortie, my little Fokker E.I had been shot up a little by stray rounds from anti-aerocraft machine-gun fire, and now would be as good a time as ever to learn how to treat bullet holes more permanently. I had also long meant to celebrate my status as an ace pilot by giving Berthe, as I call her, a fresh coat of paint.

As I stepped out onto the field, however, I saw dark shapes form from above. A horn began to sound, and I was waylaid by an engineer, who shouted, "The enemy is upon us! You must take cover!"

Then the bombs began to fall.

Sheer terror they wrought, as the enemy Caudrons fell upon the stables and hangars from out of the clouds, their bombs disabling our staff car and one or two of our Eindeckers, whistling as they went by with ear-piercing screams. It was a challenge to tell the gravity of the damage amidst the carnage, but it appeared heavy. Wood chips and dust flew everywhere, as rats fled in droves. The cat and our adoptive dogs followed suit, running about confusedly, mewling and barking as they went.

Then they turned to our barracks, keen on delivering their ordnance in such a way as to kill our men and disrupt our very living conditions. Fortunately, these bombs did little of either, as the building was reinforced and protected against such threats: the projectiles themselves were small, sixty-five pounders at most. The explosions nevertheless rent small holes in the building, and this would be sure to inconvenience us in the days to come.

All this damage I noticed in the moments after the engagement, however. At the time of the bombing, I was initially frozen in place, looking on at the carnage as the planes exposed outside the hangars fell under attack. Throwing all common sense to the wind, I decided the best thing to do would be to scatter the French assault. After running at the hangar as debris from surrounding buildings clattered down, I threw aside the chocks to my craft, spun the propeller, jumped into the cockpit, and waited impatiently for the propeller to catch so I could turn on the engine.

Buffeted to the left and right by the shrapnel and force of near misses from falling bombs, my mighty craft took to the air. Some of the other pilots rallied and followed after my example, rushing for their machines. As we slowly climbed into the sky, the enemy Caudron bombers, believing themselves outmatched, cut and ran for home. Unfortunately for them, even with their diving and weaving that sped their machines up slightly, they could not all get away unscathed. In the end, we managed to gain on a few enemy machines and shoot them down. Oberleutnant Hans Ackermann took several of the necessary shots, whilst another Caudron peeled off from their retreating formation and engaged my machine directly in a valiant rearguard action. We dueled briefly before I inevitably shot down the offending bomber, who was not accustomed to dogfighting. Nonetheless, I saluted the pilot and gunner's efforts and made a mental note to see if I could retrieve them from their machine. At this point, we were closing in on no-man's-land, where more enemy planes were likely to be hiding in wait, as this was an easy plot to enact on so cloudy a day. I turned for home, gesturing to others to do the same, but Ackermann disregarded the order, commanding two of our brethren in an ill-advised assault on an enemy observation balloon, seeming to conclude that since we were roused to duty, that we might as well avenge our aerodrome. Much to my relief, our lads were not intercepted, and the balloon went down in flames as I looked over my shoulder at their progress.

We then made for home, where we were greeted to a grim, half-hearted cheer from the ground crews. Though glad to have thrown back the bomber assault, it was with great sorrow that I regarded the ruins of my adoptive home. The stable would need to be entirely rebuilt, and there were other buildings, such as a hangar or two, that appeared to be rather badly brutalized by the bombs. What's more, the Frogs had also reduced several of our vehicles to smoking ruins. Nonetheless, the dogs ran to us, barking urgently, with many a loving lick and nuzzle, some limping along on injured legs, eager to welcome us home, even as the cat showed relative indifference—she was found hiding amongst the rafters of a bombed-out barn, toying with an unlucky rat. Most of us had survived, but an unfortunate ground crew member had been crushed to death inside the galley, having attempted to rescue a puppy trapped within the confines of the building

1 December 1915

My Diary,

As expected, Germany or France, it is cold in December. Flurries dance around our craft as our crates wait impatiently, looking to spring into the air. They will, alas for them, have some time to delay, as high command has suspended any sortieing for the time being. Nevertheless, the men wait with bated breath as they too look to the skies, afraid of another bombing raid to follow from out of the snow clouds above. Fortunately, it seems as though the Caudrons have learned their lesson. Some amongst us pilots take to it better than others and play cards and laugh. Feeling at home enough to do so, I at long last worked up the gall to kindle the lights of Chanukah. Whilst the others were out playing football and reprimanding the dogs as they attempted to interfere and take the ball for their own, I huddled myself in a corner of the common room near the barracks fireplace. There, I silently murmured a blessing over the lights and was partway through paying my respects to the holiday itself, when I heard footsteps behind me. Whirling around, I looked up to come face-to-face with the rittmeister, with a few others amongst the jagdstaffel in tow.

"Carry on, leutnant," the rittmeister remarked smilingly. "I can tell you've wanted to practice your faith for some time, and you are more than entitled to here. You fight well and have made it clear that a Jew in our jagdstaffel fills an equal place in our formation and an equal place in the grave."

I beamed inwardly.

Well then, I thought, as my fellows cautiously crowded around. "With your permission, sir," I inquired, "would you or any of the other fliegers like to help yourselves to some wine and latkes?"

There was a general murmur of casual interest as I worked my "ritual magicks" before them, and was indeed probably seen by them to be more of an actor than someone performing a sincere religious ceremony, so, in an attempt to win friends and favor, I couldn't help but include an element of drama into the rites, with great hand flourishing and projected speech in an attempt to entertain them further. The Catholics did it all the time anyway, and I daresay it was quite engaging to be seen as a sorcerer from one of the Grimm Brothers' works. Regardless, the ceremony aroused great curiosity as it continued. A number of these hardened soldiers had seen very little of Jewish life, whilst many others hadn't seen any at all. The melodious tunes and chants intrigued them, as did the Hebrew, as foreign as it sounded from the tongue of the Fatherland.

Later, as I was making a mental note reminding myself to help the cooks prepare some more food for the rest of the eight days and nights of the holiday, so successful was my "wizardry," I was pulled aside by a fellow pilot, a subordinate named Jan Schultz. He frowned mightily at me.

"I am concerned for you, leutnant."

I knew his motives at once. *Here we go*, I thought. Christian missionaries. I should have been more careful and less comfortable in the face of my squadron mates. Though perhaps I might outrank him in military command, he may well outrank me in social status. I decided to try to frighten him off.

Gritting my teeth, I hissed through them at him, "Yes, feldwebel?"

That placed him off guard! Ha! He took a step back.

"I mean no disrespect, sir," he replied, "but you do know that Jesus rewards his followers with a place in Heaven?"

"I am well aware of your beliefs to that effect, feldwebel. Thank you for your concerns."

Schultz saluted me in an overly florid manner. "Sir."

"And note that as I have always been a Jew, I shall always be a Jew."

Schultz's face fell at this, eyes wide. "You would ally yourself with the killers of Christ?"

I laughed low, confidently. Moreso than I felt, as other pilots had overheard our conversation and were watching tensely.

"I celebrate the Ancient Religion, which appeared long before Jesus—who counts as one of our own, mind you—met with his disciples. Though some amongst my number were wrong to kill your alleged Lord and Savior, there are rotten tomatoes in every faith, feldwebel. Does one stand before me?"

This was met with a roar of laughter as Schultz looked at me—disappointed, perhaps—before stomping off.

"Do not turn your back on me, feldwebel," I roared, pushing my advantage. He turned and bowed again.

"Sir," he replied, almost sadly.

2 December 1915

Perhaps in revenge for his shenanigans yesterday, Schultz may have caused me to look extremely foolish today, and while to be fair, I could have avoided the verbal sparring altogether, his words stung. I should not have had to deal with it.

On this, the second night of Chanukah, I had scored yet another two kills after a certain dearth in the shooting. The Fokker E.I is a slow device and cannot be reliably called upon to pursue retreating scout craft, so this was something of an achievement. My wingman, Herr Flieger Fritz Klinger, covered my back as I tangled with two enemy Morane-Saulniers at once and emerged victorious with little assistance. The two enemy fliers were relatively untrained and, unlike many of their fellow Frenchmen and more in a style like to British aviators, ploughed straight at me. Nonetheless, their roundels clearly said French, and so French they must be.

I returned to the aerodrome, flush with my win, and reported my successes to high command, as well as to my fellows, attempting to keep arrogance out of my voice—after all, they were but undertrained enemies—and our resident ass rained upon my parade, remarking, "We mustn't gloat, sir. It is not noble, leutnant, to bring down a pair of terrified youngsters. And between that and your weekly Friday evening . . . rituals, I can hardly call you a paragon of virtue." Even my wittiest retort, a sidelong glare, and a remark of, "Perhaps we should invite the deceased to dine on your divine patron's flesh and blood Sunday, then, feldwebel," landed poorly amidst the others. He shook his head. "Forgive him, Lord, he knows not what he says," and he departed amidst the crew's murmurs, with that bastard having carried the day for himself or not, I am unsure. I am most wroth with his ability to play a crowd and jealous of his ability to upstage me, but above all, I hate his security in his beliefs. He has no right to act that way to his superior!

Superior officer, that is.

4 December 1915

Slim pickings today in the sky. It appears the Entente is lucky.

I, however, am not. Alas, I was made the laughingstock of the squadron by seating myself upon an admittedly cleverly placed windyblaster as I took my position at the officer's mess. As there were allegedly no witnesses when it was placed, I could not discipline the individual—whom I could only assume was Schultz—for this egregious display of disrespect, and so was compelled to let the encounter go.

I suppose I should try to laugh this matter off, and I would do so much more easily if I did not suspect Schultz. It is difficult to laugh when others laugh at you, and even if some of those who laugh do so alongside you instead, it is hard to dismiss your feelings. I shall try my best to not let these days haunt my memories and be the sole recollections of my military career. There has been much good alongside these evils.

5 December 1915

I nearly struck Feldwebel Schultz today. That would teach him to go about belittling his superiors.

To give context: The skies had cleared at last after a stormy morning, but now it was deemed too cold to go flying. A certain chill had frozen the air, and it was a challenge to breathe throughout the day. Attired in our fur coats even when indoors, we shivered around the fireplace, glad that the ground crews were dutifully taking care of our craft before retiring to their quarters, as well. That night, the lads and I dined heavily off of pork, which I continued to eat, as I now felt it traditional and a bonding experience amongst the men, even as it was ritually unclean to those of my faith. Indeed, I began to realize that it was feasible, nay, almost necessary, to take a reformed approach to the faith whilst partaking in this evolving world. This amused the young feldwebel, leading me to think the situation with Schultz was over. The gentleman was duly shamed and seemed only to want to try to help raise morale with ill-placed pranks. I proceeded to bed, ushering away the dogs who had crowded themselves around my cot, seeming to cause great lumps.

Upon wrapping myself within the covers, I noticed the bed itself felt damp and covered in grease. I was unsurprised, but quite outraged, to discover the head of a pig upon a tray amidst the sheets with a placard and the words "A midnight snack for our flying Jew" written upon it. This was neither tasteful nor even acceptable, as, ritually, physically, or both, my own bed was now rendered filthy. Calling for my batman, I had him clean my bedspread before I walked over to Rittmeister Schneider's office. *At least he would not pass judgement*, I thought, as I watched the batman out of the corner of my eye whilst he balled up the sheets and went off to wash them.

My mind returned to the matter at hand as I reached the squadron leader's office. Angrier than before, I came straight to the point. "Rittmeister," I did snarl, after Schneider opened the door in a timely manner in response to my prolonged fusillade of knocks upon his office door, "Feldwebel Schultz has bespoiled my bedding!"

As I told him about the pig incident, the venerable rittmeister rolled his weary eyes. "That's Schultz, alright. Pay him no mind, Herr Leutnant. He means well. And his father has the ear of the Kaiser in military circles. Though he cannot buy his son a commission, he still wields great influence. It seems to be my only recourse to tolerate his follies for now. We do not want trouble with high command."

My eyes flashed, as my anger turned to rage, which nearly overtook me. When I caught Schneider's tired gaze, however, I realized that I was lucky. I didn't have to be responsible on the squadron's level for this pilot's abject cruelty and stupidity, and, what's more, I had not been flying alongside him for as long as the rittmeister. I should count my blessings that I had flown with largely agreeable people in the past. It was time to see what military life was like when there is a genuine nuisance, rather than merely a few wayward words tossed about, in the ranks. It was not pleasant, it was not pretty, but it will be a worthy challenge to my patience and honor. Honestly? It was to be expected in this intolerant and, considering the wartime conditions, downright xenophobic world. Maybe I would learn something and perhaps Schultz and the others would too.

I straightened myself up.

"Very well, rittmeister," I replied, voice cold, as I stared into the deep, blue eyes of my officer, which seemed to stare into my soul. "I shall tolerate our man Schultz as best I can. I understand your plight and do not wish for you to be troubled by small arguments amongst the men."

"Do not be too hard on him, leutnant. He's had a rough life."

I debated engaging Schneider on that topic. I, too, had had a hard life, much worse than Schultz's—presumably, as he wasn't targeted for genocide or pogrom. At length, I murmured this aloud to myself, and these words were picked up by Schneider's hawklike hearing. He turned to me, his eyes sensitive and apologetic.

"That is fair. Come then, bare your breasts to one another and learn to coexist."

"Jawohl."

What else could I have said? After all, when the rittmeister says jump, his pilots must merely ask how high.

If I do not put a stop to Schultz's shenanigans, however, I genuinely fear a mutiny against me and a replacement thereafter. I would think it only fair, really. If I cannot keep the men under control, they will be the undoing of my sanity and possibly my person as well. If only I could reason with this little monster, for I fear that if I continue to fail, it will be the gauntlet for him before long!

7 December 1915

At long last! A response from the British government after the *Lusitania* incident!

After weeks of worry regarding our diplomatic status with the King of England and the Kaiser's cousin, George V, the British must have recognized our valor and good intent, for even though they are our rivals in trade and naval arms races, they realize we have relative justice on our side!

Or perhaps they take both sides for fools.

Either way, neutrality is their game. The parliament of Herbert Henry Asquith has officially sworn off this war, and I thank God for it. A war with Britannia would be ruinous to our navy, as we are already fighting that of France, even as the Frogs have not stood much of a chance in the past few actions, for our dreadnoughts are doing their job well.

Ever indulging in their bullheaded nature, however, the United States, whilst likely silently thankful for our conduct during the smuggling matter, has refused to apologize and may not stand down their arms-trading game with France. This is troubling—they possess many natural resources—but they also remain at least an ocean away and are unused to modern warfare, even as they have been known to adapt their military strategies and tactics quickly. If we are able to defeat the Russians before turning our attention to the Western Front, we may yet be saved.

8 December 1915

Diary, it appears my experiences with young Schultz have me stewing with rage and unable to think of much else, even as I recognize it is unsportsmanlike and unbecoming to speak of one's allies in a derogatory manner. Nevertheless, I was, for a time, losing patience with that insufferable child. Especially as he leads his caroling choir on this, the last night of Chanukah, with that angelic and sweet voice of his, drowning out my prayers and always acting as though he's a moral paragon and getting away with all manner of terrible pranks.

It had to stop.

For this past holiday, Jan Schultz made a fool of me, and I am slowly being made to realize what an incompetent leader I am by not staunching his obnoxious behavior.

However shrouded in some perverse form of "humor," the bastard focuses all his malevolence on me, and ceaselessly batters me with his obnoxities unworthy of a noble flier, under the aegis of looking out for my "mortal soul," or "just being playful." I have written him up for disciplinary action on numerous occasions, but for all the effort I took to reprimand him, it came to naught. His father had a tight grasp over the disciplinary committees, undermining me time and time again, with the crew consistently claiming he "had the best intentions."

Command and control were breaking down in the unit. I ended up deciding to take extreme measures and paid off select individuals amongst the mechanics to help me report on the rake, hoping to catch him red-handed.

Then, tonight, a snowy, bitterly cold evening, in which the winds howled like a thousand Celtic Banshees, even as I remained safe inside, consuming freshly cooked latkes after kindling the candles for the last night of Chanukah, I received whispered word from one of the mechanics that Schultz was making his way toward the hangar where my Fokker E.I was kept. "Here he goes again," I said to myself, somewhat drained by this conflict. Pulling on my fur coat, I followed Schultz, who was bearing a bucket of red paint through the large double doors where Berthe rested. Hiding behind one of the other planes and muffling my footfalls by taking off my boots as I entered the hangar, I overheard him talking to a collection of mechanics present about his plan to paint the letters "J-U-D-E" on my machine when I decided enough was enough. Creeping up behind the ass, gesturing to the mechanics to be silent, I then suddenly leapt on him and grabbed the bucket of paint away, before sloshing it all over my hated ally. There was a certain sense of gratification at the look of shock on his face before I inquired, "How does it feel to be on the receiving end, you spoiled child? Look at you now. Were that it was your own blood! Now start behaving better, scum, or it will be your hide. I do not care what your rich old man has to say."

With a shout of rage, he came at me for this and, much to his credit, I must admit, gave me something of a pounding. One fist sucked the air out of my belly, and as I fell to my knees, another shot split my lip, spilling blood, before my valiant mechanics came to the rescue. Pulling him off me and restraining him amongst themselves, Herr Muller, the undisputed leader of the tinkerers, gave me a wink. "All yours, leutnant."

I gave Schultz my much worked upon death glare, improved in the days during which he had tormented me so. Now that he was cornered, however, I noticed him to be most unnerved, sweating, even in this intense cold. I heard a sound of running water as the poor bastard, shivering with fear, had wet himself, leaving a pool of urine on the hangar floor.

I regarded this pool haughtily, sizing it up before returning my glare to Schultz. "You were about to deface my aerocraft, sir. Beyond that, you have heaped a considerable load of disrespect upon me. Nonetheless, rather than beating the shit out of you, I shall be merciful." I gestured down at the urine. "That pool between your legs?"

He looked down, utterly humiliated.

"There is no cause to be embarrassed for shitting or urinating yourself in conditions where you brought fear upon yourself through nobility or kindness. But when you run amok in your entitled way, causing ill will toward others and are cornered for it, if you cannot own up to it and justify it, you are no man."

I smiled, my feral side coming to the fore. This was a new aspect of myself I had never seen. I very much wanted to see this fellow suffer. I advanced on him, making him feel terror. Not quite the same level of fear my parents felt during the reign of Lueger, I'm sure, but a start. It was very gratifying, but before I could truly put the fear of God in him, I stopped myself.

"Get the hell out of here," I crowed, showing ill-deserved mercy.

He stared at me blankly.

"Beat it!" I shouted.

The fucking child began to cry.

"SCRAM, YOU MISERABLE SCUMBAG!"

He scurried off like the rat he was, sniveling and bereft of dignity. I proceeded to kick him in the rump for good measure, resulting in a grunt of pain most satisfying to my ears.

"This is off the books, gentlemen," I addressed the ground crew. "If anyone speaks so much as a word to the rittmeister, I'll see them undone." I then turned on my heel and returned to the officer's cabin.

My thoughts turned to DuCoq. It had been awhile since I had thought of my noble French knight, since our time together before my release from the N73 aerodrome, and, in considering his gracious manner, wondered what he would think of me in this way. I sighed unhappily. I hope we meet once more. I miss his confident, yet humble stride and wise words. He makes me feel at home and is likely to understand these strange onrushes of violence and help me through them.

26 December 1915

My dear Diary, I had a devilishly curious Christmas this year, an experience unlike I shall ever have again.

After some rumination, I must conclude that I have gained myself a new suitor and admiration therewith from the most peculiar of individuals. It is unusual, and my parents would be furious about this development. Which part is worse? The fact that it is a man, a person outside the faith, one above me in rank and social position, or that he is from France? I do not know.

The escapade began two nights ago on the twenty-fourth, a frigid Christmas Eve, when I heard the buzzing of engines flying overhead. In the night sky, it was hard to make out, but as my eyes acclimated to the darkened horizon, I discovered a single brave little Nieuport 10 flying overhead. As the ground crews sounded the alarms and we rushed to shelter and to the gun emplacements, it seemed the machine was out of range of our machine guns and our flak missed their marks. Then it suddenly dove upon us, but neither bombs nor bullets dropped from this low-altitude attack. Instead, a strange bit of ordnance fluttered down with a FWUMP as it landed atop the officer's cabin roof and slid off one side. Curious, one of the fliegers poked at it with a stick before calling me over. I strode toward the bedeviled officer and picked up the offending item.

It was a wreath . . . a wreath with a card attached to it.

I took it inside for further examination, and noticed it was an intricately woven article with ribbons tied onto it. The card read, in beautifully inscribed German:

To our beloved rivals of the FFA 6b,

Wishing you a merry Christmas and a happy new year.
May the war end quickly, that we might meet in peace-
time in Paris.

I drink a glass to our competition and wish my
brother aviators well,

Nobly,
Your valiant foes of the Escadrille N73.

I was thankful to be alone in my quarters, studying the epistle. It was clear to me that this was no accident, and that since I had been the only guest to the Lafayette Escadrille's headquarters, that this was somehow meant for me especially. It was a delight to know that the gentlemen pilots, especially DuCoq, who I'm sure had put them up to it if he hadn't done it himself, had a place for me in his heart, enemy or no. It appears as though he had risked his life to deliver the wreath, after all! By God! What a lovely sentiment. I cannot help but raise my voice in thanks for such an understanding and considerate paramour! In Yiddish, of course, so that nobody would understand. It has been a struggle to admit it, but my appreciation for DuCoq grows ever more, outgrowing my bosom friendship with my handsome, sweet, dearly departed Ludwig, that never was quite close enough for my liking.

I sighed, and made to go to bed, when I heard a knock at my door. Much to my surprise, it was that little shit, Jan Schultz. This evening, however, his eyes were turned downwards and tearful, full of regret, his head bowed. "Leutnant, this is for you," he mumbled softly—embar-rassedly even, perhaps? "It's a gift from the unit," he continued, his cheeks reddened. I took it to be the work of the cold, until he gingerly shoved a full-sized, silver menorah into my hands. It was decorated with aeroplanes and a shamash holder modeled after an Imperial Eagle. I wondered if something was the matter, but took the moment, now that I was once more awake, to thank the crew for my lovely, if suspicious, gift. I was quick to learn that it was not as simple a matter as a mere token of appreciation for my service to the squadron. To my shock, not one of them knew of this group purchase. "It must have been Schultz, himself, leutnant," the rittmeister remarked, smiling.

"Do you think he means to pay tribute to my higher rank?" I inquired.

The rittmeister laughed. "You showed your teeth the other day, certainly. Consider it a Christmas miracle."

28 December 1915

"Sit down," said I, gesturing to a chair, one which Schultz took shakily.

Jan and I had left the barracks to go to a café to discuss the events at hand. After some amount of questioning, Schultz denied any allegations of mean-spiritedness, citing that he mostly only meant to pull me closer to Christ, "with a few playful exceptions." This angered me, but I tried to keep calm, even as I thought, *What about the aeroplane-painting incident?* Diplomacy first. He did not understand the extent of how much he wounded me emotionally. Further discussion with him revealed that he always wanted to be a churchman but his much-admired father, whom he wanted to impress, had encouraged him to join the military. Placed in the position he was, he wanted others to join him with God. I felt bad. For all my disgust toward him, he was merely lonely, and possessed, he admitted himself, of a desire to practice his passions, despite his rotten sense of humor, having never been given much attention as the middle son of a rich aristocrat. It was clear to me now that he was simply a misunderstood, but also severely underdeveloped and stupid, rich boy who did not foresee the consequences of his actions, much less seemingly make it past his early teens, when it was acceptable to play pranks on those you fancy.

Poor fellow, he promised to stop.

29 December 1915

Received a sweet little "anonymous" gift of a model figurine depicting one of our recently introduced Fokker E.III fighters in the post today. Lovely! Another gift. Not as charming nor as surprising as the first, especially as a closer look revealed a certain robes-wearing, crown-of-thorns-bearing, bearded Jewish prophet piloting it, but it was sweet! I definitely appreciated it, and my heart warmed further toward the alleged gifter. Jan denied having sent the gift but went a bit red when I gushed over how accurate the reproduction was (well, except the depiction of Jesus at the yoke). In the end, I did not really want his friendship and mainly wanted to be left alone, but I felt obligated to help a fellow flieger overcome his difficulties, and he needed help. Clearly his parentage had damaged him severely, and he was using what resources he had to compensate for his upbringing.

Or so I imagine Doctor Freud would say.

4 January 1916

I am beginning to be a little concerned about this charge of mine. He has come some way in his attitude toward me and my fellow officers and friends. He salutes smartly and cleans up his messes at last. This is wonderful news. Unfortunately, he has overshot his duties. Every day I find another small trinket in my mailbox. His intentions may be pure, but this is not the end of it. With these trinkets, letters of fawning admiration have followed, and whilst I am flattered insofar as I believe him, I know that he is not stable enough to be trusted with any manner of friendship. I shall tolerate his presence as an accomplice of war and nothing more, all whilst hoping for the conflict to end with haste, that I might be far away from him.

13 March 1916

As the green fields of France begin to show themselves once more, we take to the skies more often. Jan has, after some pushing and aided by the pull of his father, successfully had himself placed in the position of my wingman on the majority of my flights to come. I sighed upon learning of the development. This will be a long war. As we sallied forth for our first sortie together, Schultz began to show off for me, pulling all manner of stunts to express his joy in my company. I cared not for these fripperies. Our job of the day was to take down an observation balloon, so surely, we should do just that. I called him back into position by wiggling my wing madly and though he followed suit, hopefully a little embarrassed, I knew that there would be more to this matter.

I was not disappointed. Or rather, I was. There it floated. Another observation gasbag, another victim, or so it should have been. Unfortunately, young Jan, ever attempting to impress his commanding officer, or perhaps desired friend, sailed through the skies flamboyantly, attempting to catch the eye of anti-aerocraft gunners, again working his outrageous maneuvers so that they would fire on him, distracted.

The Frenchmen must have merely laughed at this pathetic excuse for a trick, however, and instead focused their fire on me, the only individual who was doing any damage to their matériel of war! This made downing the balloon much harder, and my craft was struck many times by machine-gun fire from below as I did so. Having finished the job, with the balloon receding gracelessly to the ground, deflated in a column of flame, I looked about wildly for Jan, only to find him haplessly engaged in a dogfight with a pair of Nieuports! Fortunately, so distracted were they by Jan's majestic flummery, that I managed to pounce on one, catching it off guard and engaging it in a wild flurry of bullets. The nimble, if delicate, Nieuports, however, were not to be outdone easily, and flew circles around our fighters before we were finally able to chase them off. I was so furious upon our return to our lines that I was barely able to reprimand bold Jan. Nonetheless, he took what harsh words I was able to spit out very badly, falling into some form of melancholia. I feel a tad remorseful, but realized that there is little I can do without compromising my leadership role in the squadron. What's more, he had made a mistake in the middle of a sortie—he needed to be called out in order to improve. And whilst I feel for the bastard, I do not really like him. I try to be courtly when I can be, and try to mentor him as best I can, but he should be happy he isn't demoted for the tricks, both puckish and cruel, that he plays!

Fortunately, I have decided to take a leave of absence for a time to travel to Switzerland for a few days. One of the more sympathetic fellows in my squadron has invited me to go with him and look at some art, "testing my taste" against some of the more avant-garde, supposedly downright surreal works of our time. Dadaists, I believe they are called. It would thankfully allow me to get away from our friend Schultz here, at least.

7 April 1916

At long last, this grisly matter has come to a head.

I have tried so very hard to appreciate this Jan Schultz fellow, but the bastard will not leave me alone.

Now, Diary, he has gone too far.

I thank goodness that one of our mutual companions in arms has found you, o Diary, after Jan stole you from under my pillow! Travesty! You do not steal the property of fellow pilots. This stops now!

Having called young Schultz to the airfield proper one night, I laid into him with everything I had. Politely, if presumptuously. I asked him quietly if he enjoyed my company. Tears welled in his eyes, giving him a glossy appearance in the moonlight. They glistened as he told me he had never had many friends before, certainly, but that through money and amusing others with pranks he played on the unsuspecting, he had learned to dote on those he did have, as he knew he could not carry a friendship by himself. "Indeed," said he through his tears, "and I only played the pranks on you to endear myself to you and the squadron because I wanted to save you from eternal damnation and be seen as a clever trickster whilst doing so!"

Horrifying. How pitiful and pathetic! It was like kicking a puppy, but it needed to be done.

I turned on him, fire perhaps burning a bit too brightly in my eyes. "Young man, whilst I appreciate your kindly words and compliments, you must keep them to yourself. I am a Jew, and will remain so forevermore. I will not have your bigoted father's attention drawn to me. You will cease these bold statements."

Jan's eyes narrowed. "So be it . . . Jew. I was only trying to help rescue you. Being the child of the formerly chosen people will reap you nothing before Jesus."

I raised an eyebrow, surprised by his abrupt change in humor. "Let your Jehovah judge me as he sees fit," I replied. "Your gifts were pleasant. The prospect of the attention your father will pay to the recipient is not. And let us not get into your personality."

Schultz let out a sharp bark of a laugh. "Oh, never mind the old man. He's entirely set in his ways," Schultz replied. "Is not tyranny and brutality how a man should act? As you have done to me? Though that doesn't matter anymore. I don't like you, Schaefer. Nobody does. I tried to help you, but you wouldn't listen. For all the patience God granted me, I hope he'll forgive me when I say you're not worth saving. Just be glad you outrank me . . . for now." He chortled.

I saw red. He was no Christian. He was simply using his faith to cover his own misdeeds. Reveling in excuses, as so many others had done whilst denying me fortune!

So he had learned nothing. Clearly he was lying through his teeth in the moment to gain the approval of others. He was a bored brat who merely wished to impress his father and manipulate others to his will. I turned on my heel and strode off, fighting back a desire to punch something.

"You can shove your gifts and your greedy, selfish, spoiled persona up your arse, you beastly, soiled codpiece!" I shot back over my shoulder, just as one of my fellow officers walked by. I barely noticed. "Do you really think you can stride into my personal life with a fusillade of idiotic pranks, steal my *diary*, jeopardize professional missions and both of our lives, and expect to win my affection? Your rich father may have some sway in my profession, but you will not have my friendship! Avaunt!"

I spat on the ground. "That is what I think of you, Jan Schultz. To your quarters."

His eyes darkened. "My father will hear of this, Jew. And God sees all."

"And if either comes by, the three of us will collectively have your hide," I replied curtly.

"Did I miss something?"

The other pilot had tarried a tad longer than expected in the room and was looking both amused and slightly concerned.

"Mind your own business!" Schultz and I chorused.

At least we could agree on that.

10 May 1916

As the war rambles ever onwards, I find myself in a whirlwind of engagement after engagement. I make myself scarce from Jan, who continues to wallow in some sort of perverse depression (or so he claims—he likely does it to garner sympathy from his fellows). I meanwhile throw myself into my work, garnering myself a bad reputation amongst my fellow pilots, most of whom had not heard our discussion, save by extension from Jan and Fischer (mind you, not the mechanic of the Sixty-Second FFA . . . a different Fischer, you understand), the other officer who blundered into the room near the end. I was seen as a cold fish who would abandon a friend. Occasionally I see Henri and his wingmen, and though we do our best to avoid conflict with one another, this has incurred the wrath of my allies from time to time.

Once, when flying in formation on a defensive patrol, my wingmen and I, flying with the sun at our backs, and with patchy cloud cover to boot, crossed paths with DuCoq and some of his wingmen making their way back from an attack on our observation balloons. DuCoq's machine was smoking slightly, and his compatriots were in little better repair—tattered wings and fuselages riddled with bullet holes. I could tell my wingmen were aching to finish them off and claim kills for themselves, and I could not blame them, but nor could I bring myself to see my bosom friend, perhaps lover, dispatched in the blink of an eye. I waved furiously at the direction of my compatriots, calling off any attack they had in mind. The disappointment was palpable and when we landed, old Hans Ewald sidled right up to me and let me have it, positively spitting with rage and declaring that I was conspiring to keep him from reaching his status as an ace pilot. "Why else would you protect those snail-biters from our superior arms?" he inquired of me. My only feeble response was that our mission was to defend our lines and not be drawn out of position—that DuCoq and his allies were flying home and may make it so we could not defend against future assaults against our positions. His response was to spit on the ground and walk off a few paces, grumbling. "We could have taken them and returned just as quickly," he seethed under his breath. Taking three deep breaths, he then turned to me, curtly nodded, and growled the words, "Fine, sir, fine," before stalking off.

I think that will be the end of that conflict—Ewald is a hothead but cools down after a bit—but I have to find better excuses or avoid DuCoq's aerodrome and squadron flight paths altogether. When I can, I strike down an observation balloon or a lone fighter from one of the surrounding French squadrons to make my sortie worthwhile, but, as a gentleman, I only shoot to cripple their craft, though I fly prudently, the better to keep myself alive. As I fire round after round from the cockpit of my new Halberstadt D.II biplane, I find the craft much sturdier, and decidedly swifter and more maneuverable, than my previous Fokker E.I. The enemy tends to fall quickly to the latest in our line of warplanes.

The French foeman's Nieuport 10 stands no chance, dear Diary. It was a graceful design for its time, but its time is coming to an end, and, still firing its machine gun from its top wing, it is at a severe disadvantage as both a firing platform and now for its durability. Even its maneuvering grace can be matched.

We have secured superiority over the skies for now. Currently, our only problem is having the manpower to crew and industrial capacity to crank out our warplanes and their successors at a reasonable rate to uphold this position.

It was with these thoughts in mind that I come back from a pleasurable time at home with my family back in Königsberg. It seems at last as though my mother has forgiven me for joining the air corps and decided to gift me an amulet consisting of a silver Magen David on a ribbon. "It cost me an arm and a leg, but was entirely worth it for you," she informed me. "For surely you are practicing your beliefs, are you not, my son? You are proud of your faith in the Lord?"

Afraid to incite her wrath and worried I might hurt her feelings, I assured her I am, as my father, my mother, and I dined well, considering the wartime conditions, over soups, chicken, and crackers. We drove through town in father's motor car, and I noted Königsberg to continue to be a shadow of itself. The town's buildings had certainly seen better days, and the people looked miserable—a lot more woebegone than last I had seen the area, with breadlines, and houses still in need of repair that were wrecked by the Russians. At length, a passing lorry of our soldiers came to a stop next to us and told us to move along.

Despite the hardships, it was wonderful to see my mother and father again and to know they were well. Though only my father had written to me over the past year and a half, my mother still seemed to love me as much as ever; it merely took the rekindling of relations through meeting in person to help her realize it, and what a delight it was upon doing so. The night before my return to the front, we huddled around the fireplace and exchanged fond memories, of which I had so many. It was wonderful to know that somewhere, back in Prussia, there were people who were not trying to kill me, and, in fact, cared about what little humanity remained within me.

Then I realized that I had others. Henri's kindly words were comforting to me, and I felt as though he was there for me, as was Christianne, though perhaps I should not have told her of my feelings. I'm sure most of my squadron mates, for all Jan's cruelty, did care to some extent as to my survival, and for all I knew, some may have liked me well enough. Even Ludwig, somewhere up amongst the clouds, probably yearned for my company as well.

As the days passed, however, I realized it was time to return to do my duty and, if need be, join him.

Despite the initial jubilation in seeing family once more, viewing the remains of Königsberg, such that they were, stirred up vengeful thoughts in my mind, and I looked forward to once more getting behind the controls of my craft and fighting for the autonomy of my Empire and their allies, as well as my friends and family. For a loss now would be disastrous for me, my friends, and Germany at large. In the end, I realized—my squadron mates and I—we were fighting, above all, for each other.

14 May 1916

Now that I am back at the front after a month's leave, much has changed in my absence. New planes and people dot the aerodrome, whilst once-new faces, formerly peppy and idealistic, have turned gaunt and grim as the war goes on. An attaché to the squadron picked me up at the railroad station in his motor car, his face haggard with the courier work he had been doing of late. The war has grown particularly ugly, yet it remained a deceptively pleasant day. The train I had boarded prior rattled loudly and shook wildly as I watched other, passing trains leave a trail of smoke in the otherwise cloudless sky. I attempted to strike up a conversation with an infantry hauptmann but found it difficult due to the incessant clattering of the train and the thick Schleswig-Holstein accent of the soldier in question. We were both a long distance from home, I thought, as we pulled into the station, loud blasts of artillery audible in the distance.

My welcome home was lukewarm, as only a few of the men still knew me from our prior adventures. Schneider, I had heard, had fallen in combat only a week before, and the replacement rittmeister was a harsh man, to say the least. Hailing from a Prussian military family, Rittmeister Wilhelm Wagner, not-so-affectionately nicknamed "Kaiser Wilhelm" for his domineering nature, looks upon the affluent such as myself with some disdain, believing that wealth and high birth should not only fail to command any additional respect, but should in fact be looked down upon, as they are "soft." This I learned firsthand when he scowled at my regal bearing as I stood forth to salute and meet him for the first time. Whether it was due to socialist ideologies, perhaps jealousy, having himself worked through the ranks without assistance, or maybe because he himself didn't wish to have his own authority challenged, a look at my record and paperwork, elegantly filled out to reflect my fifteen kills, changed his mind about the attitude he was showing me!

"Well then, Herr Schaefer," he remarked, scowling slightly at his mistake but not offering an apology and merely extending a grizzled paw. "Welcome back to the FFA 6b. A lot has changed since you have been gone, but I am sure an experienced leutnant like yourself will adapt. Though I'd ask that you keep our squadron drama-free. Worry not, Schultz is gone, so you don't have to be distracted anymore. I don't know what you see in him, but what you do with the contents of your pants is your own business."

What the blazes? How did they learn I looked upon men that way? I felt severely menaced and prepared to make a desperate gambit to defend what I had become . . . no . . . what was . . . me.

Then it hit me.

They assumed I carried a torch for Schultz?

"No! I would never!" I cried in disbelief, the very thought abhorrent to every bone in my body.

"Oh, is this Schaefer?" another new pilot piped up from across the hall, buzzing in for a closer look. I winced. "Yah, don't expect any promotions soon, sir. I imagine high command doesn't appreciate the work of sodomites, least of all sodomites who victimize the sons of the brass."

"But . . ."

"I guess he had a youthful look about him . . . that fae-like glimmer?" the pilot continued.

"Now listen here!" I cried in alarm. "There is nothing, nothing, between me and Schultz. Except a great deal of hatred," I amended. "Our quarrel was not of lovers, but borne of his religious bigotry. His forcing of Christianity upon me . . . whatever the reason . . . not to mention his behavior when rebuffed . . . it was galling and horrific! I will worship how I see fit! And who told you I was a sodomite?!"

For it is true I enjoy the company of men and do not care for women in an intimate fashion. (Do I care to do that with men either? Or do I just love them as people?)

And who were they to judge such behavior besides?!

There was an embarrassed silence all around before Wagner shuffled his feet. "My apologies, leutnant, but the late Rittmeister Schneider seemed to have his suspicions that Schultz confirmed, but Schneider at least wanted you to have a good leave of absence first. Schultz apparently claimed you whispered sweet nothings in his ear and struck him when he would not return his love?"

"I struck him because he was painting slurs upon my aerocraft. Without my consent, mind you, and had played many a horrific prank on me to boot!"

"And the whispered sweet nothings in his ear?"

"We whispered amongst each other once in a while because I was trying to teach him how to conduct himself properly in polite company, something his father never did!" I snarled.

"You're hardly showing such restraint right now, old boy," Wagner tutted.

"Can you blame me?" I cried, tearing up.

"That's fair. I was worried I would have to discipline you further for your alleged activity, but I am convinced I shall merely have to warn you for now. After all, Schultz's father would hardly be a fair disciplinarian and he is the next level up. He will have to be satisfied with your demotion back to feldwebel and loss of wing command until you can prove yourself responsible once more. Do not be surprised if the MPs begin poking around your quarters, too, for you are now under investigation."

I sucked in a deep breath. That hurt. My prestige, my pride, all I have worked for, gone! It was an outrage!

"Sir, I must protest. You would demote me on hearsay?"

"When it is as serious a matter as assault and alleged male-to-male romantic advances! And gifting of presents to superior officers to boot, I am told." His face fell. "My hands are tied, Schaefer. I don't know you, and this is very awkward for both of us. I'm sure you're normally a pleasant fellow, but a demotion is the best I can do. Schultz's father carries too much weight. I hope you will forgive me if we are wrong, and trust we can carry on from this messy affair. I am sure you are a man of merit and know there must be some good in you. It would behoove you to show it."

Tears welled up in my eyes. *Curse you, Schultz.*

Conducting me to the barracks, Wagner gestured to the kill board. "It seems you outstrip many a man in our squadron. I understand this is awkward, after my demotion of you, but I will rely upon you to assist me in setting an outstanding example amongst the men that will rival the discipline of every nation's best fliers, if you can," he smiled grimly. "I understand how some may think we are flying a gentleman's game, but for us, this game's penalty for losing is not insignificant. We must also regain the respect of the infantry if we are to work in cohesion with them." He cocked an eyebrow. "I have also heard of your record from the last rittmeister. By wining and dining alongside those who rain death upon our infantry, I am sure we are not doing our boys on the ground any favors! As a seasoned killer, you would agree, ja?"

I had little choice but to stare ahead and look grim as I responded, "Jawohl, rittmeister!"

I hated to do so, but I wanted no further trouble from superior officers regarding my interest in DuCoq or Schultz. My enjoyable time with one and desire to once again lash out against the other will have to wait until after the war. I need to do my job, with no frills about it.

At least the rittmeister was courtly in his dealings with me.

15 May 1916

As the rittmeister began assigning positions for the next flight, it became evident who had survived the culling to this point. Schultz was allegedly alive, but had transferred to a "less stressful" jagdstaffel, at his wealthy father's demand!

That bastard, manipulating rumors to land himself a cushier place at the front.

As long as he stays away from me.

Between casualties and transferals, the remnants of my original squadron numbered only five pilots, varying in skill, rank, and ability, though backed by reinforcements, bringing their total numbers back up to twelve. It is tiring, attempting to re-form friendships and find those I once called my friends had moved on somewhat in my absence and formed protective cliques, especially since the debacle with Schultz. Fortunately, few who knew both of us take him seriously. Unfortunately, making the acquaintances of new pilots is more challenging. Though they are more open-minded in their desperation to cozy up to people they know, they are decidedly unwilling to cozy up to an alleged sodomite, and many shy away at the sight of me. Nonetheless, there are some who seem to worship me for my ability to kill—a concept I find a tad disconcerting.

Amongst the commissioned-officer corps, a demographic no longer including myself, we have the rittmeister, an oberleutnant, and three leutnants. Of these, Oberleutnant Jacques LeRoy, a Jewish refugee in the face of French anti-Semitism following the Dreyfus Affair, now a German citizen and former university student, is a bookish intellectual, not unlike Otto, more concerned about administrative efficiency than flying. He seems to appreciate me, and I, him. We also appear to share an interest in horticulture, and indeed first met one fateful morning as he was gathering flowers in a small garden he was cultivating. I was struck by the beauty of the various plump cherries and tomatoes and, starved for conversation, asked how best to grow them, wondering if perhaps it would behoove me to learn how to grow my own food. In the conversation that followed, I must have impressed him, as he hoped to take me on as an apprentice, so that we might raise vegetables and fruits to help serve at squadron dinners.

Unfortunately, the war must also be seen to.

Indeed, nowadays, it seems some American citizens want to play at war a time.

A sizable cadre of volunteers have flocked to what has been termed an "Escadrille Lafayette," a French-equipped, French-instructed, mostly American-crewed unit named in honor of a French hero who stood by the Americans in their war of independence. Clearly America's close relationship with France and debt to her for their having helped win independence from Great Britain has resulted in the newly sworn allegiance of idealistic schoolboys and crazed daredevils to la Belle France.

Whom we shall engage in combat.

As many German states quarreled with them once, fighting against their Continental Line in their revolution, we shall do so again. Somehow, we must rout the American volunteers from the field, yet gently, such that they might not return with more planes and men to avenge their losses with the full brunt of their government at their beck and call.

Though the concept of fighting the entirety of the United States of America should cooler heads not prevail remains frightening, my feelings were assuaged somewhat by the pitiful flying capacities of these Lafayette pilots on their first patrol. Equipped with top-of-the-line Nieuport 11 "Bébé" fighters, these extremely graceful sesquiplanes, thanks to my modicum of skill and a little bit of luck, were no match for my relatively clumsy Halberstadt D.II because those piloting the Nieuports fought so poorly.

As the Yanks confidently flew in an unbroken formation, I took to the clouds and soared far above them with the sun at my back. The American pilots, three in number, remained blissfully unaware of my maneuver, as the sun was in their eyes. Signaled by my new wingman, one of our new transfers, Vizefeldwebel Philipp Mayer, that he would stay above and watch for trouble, I dove upon the enemy, leaving Mister Spandau to do the rest.

Noticing one of their aeroplanes being shredded and eventually felled from the rear, "les autres bébés," an apt description for both my enemies and their craft, tore off in different directions, breaking formation in great disorder. It was then that Mayer made *his* attack run, following in my footsteps. Failing to communicate his intentions to his partner, one of the panicking Nieuport 11s dove downwards to the safety of friendly lines at a speed my Halberstadt could not follow, but this only deprived his ally of safety as my target's other friend, emboldened, perhaps enraged, by his fallen wingman, lost his composure and turned to meet my challenge. Hotchkiss bullets sang as I attempted to dive beneath the attack, but to his credit, the foe used his nimble aeroplane to great effect, matching my every move until Mayer smashed him from behind.

All too easy.

If this is all the Americans can offer, then may they come at us in droves. They fly like stillborn kittens and deprive the more skilled Frenchmen of their own craft, as the United States government, still neutral, has furthermore yet to make their own machines of any quality.

But in greater seriousness, may their display of ineffectuality dissuade President Woodrow Wilson and his cronies from entering the war. We do not need more enemies, of which we have plenty. This conflict has undermined the goodwill of many cultures and cancelled the Summer Olympic Games which was promised to us for hosting purposes.

I am disturbed to note that DuCoq is no longer anywhere to be seen. Indeed, I have not seen many French pilots in our sector recently, and it worries me. Did Henri's Escadrille N73 transfer elsewhere without my knowledge? *Idle worries*, I thought. I am concerned, however, that perhaps he is waiting for the right moment to surprise and make contact with me, having bypassed the defenses of my allies. It would be unfortunate, as I would be pressured to strike him from the sky.

And as I am unsure I could bring myself to shoot him down, I could well be a dead duck.

The oberleutnant calls. It is time for us to engage in some horticulture!

20 September 1916

Autumn is all but upon us once more, Diary, as the war in the air continues to be fought marginally better by the Central Powers than by the Entente. Despite our relatively greater share of the victories, however, our embattled lads must improve their abilities if we are to win overall, as, again, we of the Central Powers do not have the combined industrial capacities and manpower of the Entente. Fortunately, having noticed the exploits of private American citizenry in the air on the side of the French, the British, seeming to wish to lengthen the war, presumably as to continue to sell arms to both sides, have rushed to the aid of us, their German cousins in blood, once more balancing matters in some small capacity.

Well, not so much their government, nor the Royal Flying Corps, but, like the Americans, individual volunteers from Britannia have been finding their way to the front in a small but substantial trickle of manpower. These bright-eyed, bushy-tailed chaps are joining ground crews, serving as batmen, and slowly learning the ways of flight through these positions in their off hours, hoping to fly for us before this "war to end all wars" is concluded. I, myself, have been asked to offer endorsement to a number of prospectives, and have granted a few my blessing, allowing them to be trained at our facilities behind friendly lines. As a rather storied pilot, regardless of my . . . quirks, I am responsible for them, so I live in terror of their possible incompetence.

Fortunately, my new hobby keeps me from spending too much time worrying. Oberleutnant LeRoy, who studied biology at one of our universities and is a longtime resident of Saxony, has greatly improved my already formidable theoretical understanding of gardening. Together we plant, fertilize, and water cherries and tomatoes alongside the hedges of the aerodrome, driving the rittmeister mad. As we work the land, we converse, drinking lemonade as we weed. As I discuss with him statistics and tips on flying our craft, he confides in me the horrors of the Dreyfus Affair, the aftereffects of which drove him and the Jewish population of France into a state of great consternation. It made me wish I could hate the French, but I realize that there was still DuCoq, his brothers in the N73, and surely others, who were worthy of respect.

The rittmeister is never fond of our activities. "Stop with the landscaping, you sentimental fools!" "Kaiser" Wilhelm cries, thrashing his cane in the air. "There is a war to be fought."

"And we cannot focus on it with precision unless we have opportunities to relax!" I shout back, waving merrily, enjoying my gardening with my friend. Wagner has yet to find a response to that.

There is talk of another push of the infantry in coming days, and we will be needed to provide close support to our allies on foot. We've been flying defensive patrols of our section of France, territories gained some time ago, and this new assault comes as a welcome turn of events. It will not be an easy fight, but if the lads keep formation when called to, and stay sharp, I am sure we will do well! We smile to each other, perhaps somewhat ruefully, about the havoc we are about to cause, knowing that this is a life-or-death matter, and nothing personal in nature.

Indeed, the concept of allowing myself to be called upon to carry out such a dangerous and cruel mission as strafing somewhat helpless enemy infantry in defense of our own is galling and gives me pause. Unfortunately, I have no real friends in the squadron besides the oberleutnant to complain to, and it seems as though no nation truly appreciates the Jewish perspective on matters, let alone my own, as most of my squadron mates still distrust me for the horrific rumors Schultz gave rise to whilst I was away on leave. In the end, I must make a living, and the living I excel at is war. So war I shall. For my own preservation.

When we sally forth, it is all but assured that the enemy will return fire from above as well as from below as we speed by at low altitudes, guns blazing too quickly to keep track of bullets or accuracy. Though it will cover the advance of our beleaguered army, which has been pounded by enemy shot and shell and forced to abide in appalling conditions for inordinate amounts of time, I am sure they will be no safer in their charge across no-man's-land and will suffer terrible losses in the teeth of French defensive fire. I hope that they do not see it as our fault: a distinct possibility, as it is because of our presence in the vicinity that high command has grown so bold as to order the attack!

22 September 1916

Diary, in a single, cruel twist of fate, an early victory in this war has been snatched from our grasp.

Though our initial attacks gained a great deal of ground with the assistance of our storm troopers in an early morning assault on the enemy, after which we reinforced these shock troops with line units, our progress soon ground to a halt as the French received new men, and Moroccans, no less, to plug the gaps in their lines. These dark gentlemen, utterly devoted to their colonial masters, fought like the devil himself to hold the line against our repeated assaults, devastating our numbers on the ground, even as we scored several victories from the air and did our utmost to suppress the enemy's entrenchments and blind their artillery with the destruction of their observation balloons.

Whilst we largely control the skies, our infantry assaults, having bogged down in the face of chattering machine-gun fire, give the French a grave advantage on foot. It was, in fact, whilst defending our retreating men from the Moors that the unthinkable happened.

That fateful day, I, my crate gifted with a new green coat of paint, Oberleutnant LeRoy, and Vizefeldwebel Mayer, were on a patrol of these lines, Mayer leading our wing such that he could fill the position more regularly when the time came. It wasn't long before we caught sight of a French scout wing diving to strafe our infantry, the better to support a counterattack on our forces. The French screamed downwards at a nigh terminal angle, their wings almost shedding in the speed of their descent, doing their utmost to do the most possible damage to our men whilst also engaging one of our observation balloons with a terrifying new weapon of which I had heard tell but had not yet seen in action.

The Le Prieur rocket, when set off, danced and gamboled, scream-ing through the skies with a nigh unparalleled ferocity and utter unpredictability that, with its explosive capacities, struck fear into the hearts of our drachen pilots and crewmen. Though wildly inaccurate, they tended to be fired in volleys and a successful hit was met with a jolly explosion. And now they intended to use it against these brave, unarmed observation ballooners? I think not!

With Mayer in the lead, we accordingly focused on these attackers. As we neared, I noticed the American Indian sigils painted on each plane, clearly marking them members of the Lafayette Escadrille. To their credit, these gentlemen saw us descending from the skies and broke off their attack runs, though not before having reduced our drachen to a blazing inferno as it fell to the earth.

Damn! High command will not be pleased!

They cast themselves and their newfangled Nieuport Bébés about the battlefield, climbing and looping and giving our now seemingly rather clunky Halberstadts a terrible time. Their crates were more delicate and continued to suffer from the design flaw involving their guns mounted on their upper wings, but were even more maneuverable than the very graceful and speedy Nieuport 10s! Our formation suffered many bullets to our fuselages, before our young vizefeldwebel went down, gouts of smoke streaming from his crate before his machine burst into flames.

God damn it all! The loss of another promising pilot!

I pounded my machine's dashboard, gnashing my teeth in rage and in disbelief, blaming myself for our losses—for it was under my partial supervision that our gallant young charge fell in combat. As I raged, however, it was not long before I realized two more Nieuports had screamed from the skies above us. Mourning our losses had to wait. This was a trap!

In the pitched dogfight to follow, it was clear we were outmatched, if by number alone. The Nieuports swam around us, like, I am told, to the sharks of the ocean, awaiting their attack on bloodied prey. We did our best to crawl back to our base, bruised and battered, but fight-ing two-to-one odds in slower, clumsier machines made things diffi-cult. Fortunately, the oberleutnant was not one to die easy. As LeRoy gestured me back to our lines, we two Jews in arms dove low, just above the trees. One of the enemy pilots attempted to follow suit and received a green belly for his efforts, tangled amongst the trees behind our lines. Looking behind me, I noted two of the other scouts breaking off their attack, whilst a third, one from the surprise attack on our rear, cruelly continued the chase.

As I spotted the enemy pilot's Nieuport coming up on us quickly, I swung my Halberstadt around, cringing as the machine creaked. Realizing our respective gun platforms and the toughness of our fuselages measured out in favor of Imperial Germany, I jousted the bastard, narrowing my eyes in concentration as I spewed hot lead at his craft. He returned fire in kind, seemingly a little jarred that I had the gall to engage him, and the duel was on.

At first, it did not look good for me. My engine sputtered at every turn, and I tried in vain to keep up with the turns of my enemy and could only watch helplessly as my opponent traipsed about in a manner suspiciously familiar in hindsight, but not something I could pick up in the heat of combat as he playfully pumped my crate full of lead. As we crossed over a stretch of plains, I considered crash-landing, but for all I knew, this could be a pilot who shot downed enemies for fun! I had best be on the defensive. Desperately throwing my plane all over the sky, I nearly ended up colliding with the oberleutnant.

The oberleutnant!

Thank God.

My eyes went wide in surprise as LeRoy took on the American, or perhaps fellow Frenchman, spitting bullets from his Spandau with great accuracy, right over my own machine, using me as cover. A ruthlessly efficient approach, but he had the shot and I did not. The enemy fell in flames. A job well done, to say the least!

This joy, however, was short-lived. As we returned to the front lines, we saw our trenches, and indeed, all our gains for the day, overrun. Even our observation balloon was destroyed. Our men were in retreat, the enemy, too exhausted to pursue.

With the day lost, we returned to our miserable barracks to report a failed operation.

Only the next day, after confirmation of the kills had come through and the bodies inspected, did we learn that one of our pursuers from the Lafayette Escadrille was, in fact, none other than the dashing Frenchman and the gentleman who initially inspired me to become an aviator, Monsieur Henri DuCoq, a major formerly serving in the Aviation Militaire. He had been reassigned to train the new American reinforcements and was indistinguishable from his allies in his new plane with new markings, made more complicated by the fact that he had not seen me in a Halberstadt before.

Upon hearing the news, I returned to my bunk and wept. I could have *killed* Jacques for striking down DuCoq! It took me some time to realize that he was only doing his job fighting a war of vindication, justifying his existence as a German citizen and meritocrat, having come from a land choked in anti-Semitism.

Just like me.

And, of course, I had to realize too, that the counterattack . . .

It was my idea.

I was the killer.

27 September 1916

It has not even been a week since the death of my beloved foeman and much has changed at the front. I should like to grimly report, dear Diary, that I have been restored to the rank of leutnant and for this dark achievement somehow gained the respect of the squadron. A Second-Class Iron Cross medal bestowed upon my breast by high command has not hurt my prospects either. My score now stands at twenty-seven confirmed aerial victories as I have been patient and prudent, and, though rarely wishing to kill my foes, sometimes the enemy has left me no choice and I have been compelled to defend myself with great spirit. In the end, perhaps I should be proud of my achievements. I did, after all, yearn to restore myself in the esteem of my fellow pilots, if only to prove myself better than them.

I certainly was not. Neither proud of my achievements nor likely better than all of them.

Possibly luckier.

DuCoq was gone, and many of his virtuous Frenchmen, brothers in his crusade, no matter how cruel their government, were disgusted at my actions, almost as horrified as I was in committing them. To make amends, I attempted to drop a wreath from my aerocraft upon the runway of their base but was met with fusillades of anti-aerocraft fire. When I refused to shoot back, they fired at me still. It was clear they were in no mood to talk. This sentiment was exacerbated when several American pilots, mentees to DuCoq, flew overhead, raining threatening letters expressing a desire to hunt me down in particular.

The only bright point in all of this is that, after suffering greatly over the course of these difficult past months, I received word that I was acquitted for my accounts of assault, as Jan Schultz's overbearing father had read his diary and learned of the indignities his son had visited upon me. With high command restoring my initial promotion, as I noted earlier, I was, in fact, soon after made an oberleutnant with the latest promotion, and at last began to win over my formerly suspicious squadron mates. Despite the support of my comrades, I felt uneasy—not for my own life, but for that of my allies who, at long last, cared about me enough to want to defend me. It appears the Franco-American alliance now deems me a wanted man and will do anything to see my crate's propeller mounted on their barracks wall as a war trophy. As I noted, this puts my squadron mates in danger, and though they are not all my closest friends, many have sworn their loyalty to me, and I to them, and I have gotten to know some of them well as true mensches. I would hate to see them gunned down on my behalf.

Perhaps it is time to transfer. I can choose a new squadron, far from here, with a new plane, and under whose aegis I will fight without fear of recognition.

Let the Americans call me coward for running from the front after gunning down their beloved leader. I have larger matters to attend to than a fragile ego.

1 November 1916

Diary,

After some wallowing in my sadness, having felt somewhat at home with my former squadron, I have concluded, pending an accepted application, that I will join the Jagdstaffel von Knyphausen, based near the commune of Bertincourt, France. They need competent pilots—or so their oberleutnant, one Stefan Kirmaier, advertised—to rally and inspire their new recruits, and said that it was here I could get a fresh start, namely by fighting a different collection of American units in a different region. My new unit, as its name suggested, being the namesake of a Hessian hero in the British Army during America's War of Independence, is crewed almost entirely by English civilians, here to assist their allies in a time of need (as Lafayette helped the Americans). Nevertheless, despite the inexperience of our English allies, the experience of helping them against Americans would be "like shooting clay ducks on a weekend," the rittmeister, Kirmaier, wrote, his arrogance oozing with his every word, "for the Americans fly like shit, and whilst the English staff of our squadron are little better, they are more decisive in their actions. This means a lot in combat," he wrote. "Many of our rookies in the jasta show bravery," he continued. "We simply need veterans to teach them how to use this trait."

A chance to continue the fight without a bounty to my name?

A chance to meet new, possibly friendly people?

A chance to inspire the next generation of aviators?

I jumped at the opportunity! Perhaps this was for the best. I mourned DuCoq, but to have a fresh start may be exactly what I need.

22 January 1917

Diary, it appears the American government has waited long enough to watch the war ride itself out without them. At long last, they have picked a side.

The Entente's.

Just as I feared. After the wholesale slaughter of the early volunteer expeditionary force of idealistic college students and daredevil racer pilots joining the ranks of French and Russian fliers, it seems as though American President Woodrow Wilson has, under great pressure, reluctantly upped the stakes to prove a point—you cannot kill an American and get away with it. It did not help that the Russians, in an uncharacteristic effort at skullduggery rather than brute-force, forged a telegram replete with information that Mexico was in league with our nation the better to topple the United States. It appeared our friendly neutrality toward the Americans, even the sparing of the *Lusitania*, has not paid off, as the Yanks cometh, hoping to bring their navy to bear to harass and undermine the British mercantile convoys bringing volunteers and supplies to Germany and Turkey, perhaps slipping in troops of their own to supplement the French and Russians on their respective fronts. Fortunately for us, the Russians have begun to falter, their peasants groaning under the strain of wartime exhaustion as our most elite guard units strike home. I understand we may soon be able to transfer some of these men and bring them to bear against the French and Yanks in due time, and that excites me.

Rather grotesquely so, as I should not be cheering for the downfall of a nation, even one whose people oppose the very existence of my own.

In the meantime, our squadron has been shredding the enemy over the Somme. My fellow German officers and our English charges rally under my command with the unfortunate passing of Oberleutnant Kirmaier, who foolishly flew alone and tangled with a pair of ancient, but desperately flown, British-made, and American co-opted Airco DH.2s.

So much for the "shitty" quality of American fliers.

My steady veteran hand, if not overly charismatic tongue, carries the day much of the time. However, I shall not deny that I am greatly assisted by the calculating technique of a meteorically rising Leutnant Manfred von Richthofen. This fellow, a student of the late Oswald Boelcke (the aviator I met whilst hospitalized), was initially a cavalry officer, just like Ludwig. Now, though still a mediocre pilot, he listens to instructions and executes the maneuvers with grace, if not creativity. He is also a dead shot. Boelcke, also recently struck from the cockpit alongside Kiermaier with many more of our ilk besides, may have fallen, but despite these losses, through American miscalculations and our once more superior craft, some of our men make ace with relative ease, and together, we endure. Our brotherhood is courtly and well-intentioned, polite, perhaps, but not that friendly—the English volunteers tend to be aristocratic, keeping to themselves—but we are all bound closely by our survival instinct. We are a cohesive team, even if our interactions outside the battlefield and briefing rooms are mostly limited to nods of acknowledgement and small talk. I could see how my combat record would seem intimidating—I know I used to think similarly of my officers—but I have always attempted to be anything but a killing machine. And yet, I am a pilot. It is my job.

3 April 1917

Today I am called upon to perform an entirely new mission. A diplomatic one on behalf of our propaganda corps. I find the envoys from the media to be insufferable. They are everything I was—idealistic dreamers without a brain amongst them who would simply not listen.

That was their greatest failing of all.

Today, they presumed to storm our aerodrome and have us film a moving picture with them that would push individuals to join the Imperial German Air Force. That was well, but they were impeding on our territory without our permission.

"Come now," they said. "We are trying to help! We wish to cover the heroics of our most noble, gallant air corps! Don't you want more enlistments?"

"No," Richthofen replies simply, before turning his back on them and returning to work in the hangar, adjusting his gun sights, and leaving me to stave off the masses alone.

"So, Mister . . .," they began, glaring in my direction.

"Atkinson. Darius Atkinson," comes a voice from behind me. I whirl around.

One of our usually soft-spoken and more cautious fliegers, English by extraction, had dashed onto the scene to save my neck and proceeded to speak on, addressing the film crew.

"I have been delegated to speak on behalf of the rittmeister and his crew. Most of us are very busy, don't you know, and you should be too, doing your bold, noble, media handiwork rather than wasting your time with us, the base, filthy, dogs of war." This elicited a laugh from me.

The crew wasn't amused. "Why can't we speak to your leader? He's right here!" They pointed at me.

I faux-innocently pointed to myself and mouthed, "Me?"

Darius interceded. "He has laryngitis. Let him be!"

There was some grumbling at that.

"Now, now," Darius replied. "Fortunately for you, we do want enlistees, just as you want stories. Let us compromise."

So we went along with it. They wined us, dined us, and provided a very flattering account of our adventures, whilst we performed for their movies in their crowd-pleasing ways—stunt-wise for the battle scenes, pulling great loop the loops and newfangled barrel rolls and acting more as daredevils would, rather than actual combat aviators, even as they did not let us portray our own roles on the ground, relying on actors instead. What kind of slap in the face was that? Our fliegers would never conduct ourselves in the fashion of these melodramatic saps who now pollute our headquarters! We endured three days of this filming before they went on their merry way, leaving us a tad disgruntled, but with high hopes for support from home.

In the meantime, Atkinson's quick thinking was rewarded, and he became the first Briton in our squadron to be commended for noncombative valor. *It won't be long before he makes feldwebel*, I thought, as I invited him to join the officers in a game of bocce.

12 August 1917

Today I have struck from the sky my thirty-fifth kill, an eight-kill ace by the name of Jean-Paul Renault. From the cockpit of my extremely maneuverable Fokker Dreidecker 1 scout, the hapless fellow was alas, an easy target, strapped suicidally to a Nieuport 24, an experimental craft now proven, at least by this engagement, to perform only a little better than a Nieuport 17 and unable to keep up with our arms race. Thanks to the cruel missteps of French engineering and a victim to his government's folly, his lone-wolf patrol was cut short as I fell upon him, attempting to strafe his craft just enough to render it inoperable.

Soon after my victory appeared imminent, I recognized his predicament and attempted to disengage. In the true style of a chivalric knight, however, the fellow would not yield, and when I attempted to turn my back, he less nobly stitched my plane so full of ordnance that my engine began to stutter. That would not do! As my plane stammered in protest, I quickly attempted an Immelmann turn, in which I climbed with what speed I had, all whilst coming about in his direction. There, to the entertainment of the troops on both sides of no-man's-land below, we jousted again, and I could only imagine the soldiers in the trenches betting amongst themselves who would come out atop. Today, I did. My shots struck home along his wings and struts, just as he, recognizing the danger of our engagement, lost his nerve and broke from further engagement. This stress his plane could not bear and, like to a molting swan, its struts buckled, the wings collapsed, and he and his machine tumbled to the earth.

31 October 1917

Diary,

With the harvest season concluded and a certain darkness beginning to pervade the land, I believe the time has come to raise morale amongst my contemporaries. At the behest of high command, it has fallen to me to provide entertainment for the infantry division staff stationed in our vicinity, as well as the pilots of our and four surrounding squadrons. Local women were to be included as well. In catering to so many soldiers, not to mention officers, calling for wine, women (or rather, additional women!), and song was necessary, but they had to be used judiciously. A dance sounded excellent, but the Viennese waltz and forms akin to it were all but passé. Scouring the ranks of those invited, I found a single American mechanic who knew his way around a modern-day dance floor and bid him to teach the lads and lasses the ways of new dance forms—the foxtrot, animal dances, and ragtime—to lend to the party experience. Surely if he could make our aeroplanes dance, it stood to reason he could make us do so too!

It was not quite so easy.

The lessons proceeded well, with our skilled pilots comprehending the new steps, certainly. The refreshments, too, some of which were ordered in from Germany, others, from occupied bakeries in France, went down pleasantly enough. Unfortunately, I should have asked for permission before inviting the mechanics, who always seemed to form a different clique and whose favor I wished to curry.

Scandal ensued.

Because they were explicitly invited, there was nothing high command could do to tell them they were not invited. However, the brass were *not* pleased, and made it a point to snub the mechanics at every turn, with many women refusing to dance with them, officers refusing to talk to them, and people mistaking them for waiters. Fights broke out as a result, and the party was over almost as quickly as it had begun, with the military police called in to stem the chaos.

The financial casualties for that hour of dance were outrageous, but at least our squadron was permitted to keep and eat the leftovers.

1 November 1917

Diary, this may be the last you'll see of me. For on a less than fantastic note, I was called out to a duel for defending one of my mechanics. The poor fellow was at the party and, whilst there, was slighted by a young woman whose honor, she felt, was in turn slighted by him for asking her, a noblewoman and daughter of a duchess and brigadier general, to dance. Her honor was, in turn, defended by a leutnant of the next squadron over, one Kurt Ahlefeldt. I know him for being a six-kill ace and a dangerous and aggressive warrior who flies more like a Briton, if not a very bright one, than a German.

The way my mechanic friend, Johannes Schmidt tells it, and I believe him, the woman turned up her nose to him when he asked her to dance, but said something whilst doing so, and he couldn't quite catch her words over the band. As he stole closer, asking her for clarity, she felt threatened and screamed, leading to the first punch to be thrown by the "heroic" Ahlefeldt at Schmidt, cracking his jaw. From there the general scuffle ensued. I broke up the original bout by pinioning Ahlefeldt's arms behind his back and demanding he stop this senseless bloodshed, and he demanded formal satisfaction.

Fortunately, in a way, Ahlefeldt's sense of pride would not allow him to sully himself by dueling a commoner, even if he would attack one outside of such a bout (where's the honor in that?), so he demanded I stand in for my comrade, assuming that, as a pilot, I was a gentleman. Eager to take him and his assumptions and aristocratic nature down a notch, I remarked that I was happy to do so, not thinking of the consequences, such as death or punishment, having learned afterward that dueling was also highly illegal.

Now I, with no formal training in sabre, save for some basic foot-work, thrusts, and slashes taught to me by Ludwig in years past, am about to sally forth and meet my fate.

Were that Ludwig were still alive, and not just to stand in for me!

2 November 1917

Well, Diary, as the sun rises the next morning, I greet you as the victor. It was a close affair, but I made out alright.

Namely, by default.

After spending the night practicing my lunges and advances, my parries and ripostes, my flèches and balestras, courtesy of my second and fellow Jew, LeRoy, whose father by chance taught the art of the sword in a salle in the city of Orléans, it was decided that the matter was hopeless and that I had best make preparations for the afterlife or a continued existence of dishonor. I approached Ahlefeldt's aerodrome, mighty, imposing, and foreboding, around five thirty in the morning for our six o'clock duel. Upon seeing my opponent in this distance, trussed up and strutting like a peacock, I noticed he and the surgeon, called upon to care for our inevitable wounds, were not alone, and in fact had been accosted by the aerodrome military police! Beating a hasty retreat, I later learned that LeRoy, whom I had named my second, had, in advance, summoned the constabulary on my foeman for calling me out to this duel, allowing me to both keep my honor (as I did not shirk from battle, so much as my foe was detained ahead of the time I was to arrive) as well as stay within the realm of the law! Oh worthy friend!

Of course, it will always be a matter of suspicion that I, a scheming, duplicitous shylock, might have orchestrated the perfect downfall of the leutnant, but I assure you, Diary, that is not the case. I am as innocent as a spring lamb.

Who kills for a living.

4 November 1917

Those dastardly Americans.

As if I have not been castigated for my beliefs enough, now they are manipulating my people, the Jewish people, to war against my fatherland? I am disgusted, to say the least. This is most foul play!

Diary, the so-called Palestine Declaration has just been announced by a joint government exercise in manipulation by the Italians, Americans, and French to the world, to better ensure the Jews a nation of our own. Extremely opportunistic of President Wilson, one of the foremost proponents of this plan, as we know well his anti-Semitic and racist tendencies.

They presume to gift us—without the consent of its owners, mind you—Palestine, long alleged to be our ancestral homeland. It is land, and it would have been a worthy gift, were it not so much an underhanded one. People already live there! Who are we to displace these individuals who have long inhabited the land in our absence since the Kingdom of Judea? And why should we, being German Jews, wish to upset the delicate balance in the lands belonging to our allies, the Ottoman Empire?

Ah, that's right—it doesn't matter to the French, Americans, and Italians what we think. They merely want to play us off the Central Powers, then, in Wilson's case at least, move us out of their respective countries to Palestine en masse and bill it as a victory for humanitarianism.

Further *still*, individual Jewish citizens had already been in talks with Turkey, who had offered private land to us Jews in a financial transaction years before and would likely, rightly, expect us to protect them as part of their ailing, but still somewhat expansive empire. They would be loath, I imagine, for a number of reasons, to simply give up the land without a fight, and I bet that a bellicose response to the Entente's declaration is exactly what Wilson and his team are hoping for.

By doing this, the Americans will be stirring up hatred against the Central Powers, and sowing distrust amongst all those Jews serving with them. Even as I am moved to rage and entirely unconvinced by the "generosity" shown by the American forces and their allies, distrust is successfully woven toward me amidst my once somewhat religiously tolerant men, and I begin to feel all the more uncomfortable about being at their head. Mutters and whispers abound about me working for the other side, and I feel a need to stop further teaching or showcasing my beliefs.

Honestly? I am offended that people would believe that I would defect simply because another nation's leadership offered me and my people a country of our own. Germany, for all her phobias and distrusting citizens, always has protected me and has been a strong and comforting fatherland. She has sheltered me from the nationalism and the anti-Semitism of Austria-Hungary, as well as Russia's wrath. She has found me many friends, and, after some thought since Pesach past, I have concluded that I do not need a nation of my own people fighting alongside me to feel comfortable. We have moved on since our times of bondage in Egypt. We are all Germans first, and men of our respective religions second. Is that not enough? Besides, there is a certain beauty in cultural diversity. One learns, evolves, and comes to their own conclusions through it. I, personally, do not see a need for Palestine to be warred over like the Jews and Philistines once more. The Turks currently administer to a small population of Jews in Palestine as is and treat them with passing respect. We do not need to inconvenience them further. It is not our land to steal.

Let us also face facts. Do we Jews *desire* Ottoman land? Their government is already in a state of upheaval thanks to a revolution of Arabs in their lands and, worse, a civil war, with the so-called "Young Turk" movement, a force of reformation whose views of modernization and nationalism were all very well in some respects, but who also opposed our influence on their empire. Led by a band of conspiratorially inclined medical-school students, our spy rings purport that they are backed by the French, many of their supporters having fled to Paris when Sultan Abdul Hamid II first attempted to repress them. The Turks fight gallantly, but their armies are undersupplied and so divided, I sometimes wonder why we drag them with us into battle, only to remember they have the Russians distracted, whilst they now have engaged the Americans and French as well.

Fresh from downing my third American-crewed DH.4 (by GOD do the British like to profiteer from selling both sides aerocraft in this war) in as many days, I have decided to act on the subliminal message half the squadron seemed to be offering me. Apparently, I must prove myself an even more worthy ally to Germany, and be willing to turn against the very Jews who are my brothers.

So be it. I shall sally to the Middle East and face the Jewish Legion and whatever other minions General John "Black Jack" Pershing, a decorated veteran of many American wars and appointed commander of the Palestine front, throws at us.

It will be a pilgrimage, I think. *Perhaps I shall regain some faith in my religion.*

Or so I hope.

30 January 1918

And so, I have picked up my belongings and made the move to Egypt, joining Three Filo, stationed in the vicinity of the Sinai Peninsula. My compatriots in Europe, relatively new to my acquaintance, were pleased to see me go. "Not," one noted, "because you are a bad man, but merely because you have inadvertently painted a crosshairs on all of our machines." This was fair. In addition to my own desire to leave the region to avoid the fallout from the Palestine Declaration, so egregious was the loss of Henri DuCoq to the Americans that word had spread to even the newly arrived regional Yankee Doodle pilots that the German ace Maxwell Schaefer, who had hunted their Lafayette Escadrille predecessors, had entered their sector. This made the Yanks all the more aggressive, each pilot intent on targeting my craft. Losses on both sides had mounted, both on the land and in the air, though we had the lead in kills regarding both, especially with the introduction of the British "land ship" that, whilst susceptible to artillery, broke through the enemy ranks like a bull through china. America's population of pilots and planes, not to mention soldiers and field guns, outweighed ours in this sector, especially when factoring in their allies.

Unable to help them, I found myself a prisoner of luxury, sent forth on the Orient Express by means of Munich, Vienna, Budapest, and Bucharest toward Istanbul. Along the way, I rubbed elbows with great officers and celebrities, discussing tactics and strategies, as well as art and horsemanship over wine and fine dining, a far cry from the grim, ghastly, bone-jolting, and cramped troop transport conditions.

Along the way, as I said, I found myself once more in Austria-Hungary. Back in the lion's den from whence I was once sprung.

Memories long forgotten abounded in my mind as I bore witness in my brain to the derisive shouts of the Viennese citizenry, swords, torches, and pitchforks in hand, driving away my people. To say I was on edge was an understatement.

That being said, when I arrived in Vienna, I was heralded as a hero! Photographs were taken of me; people cheered my name and bought me drinks. Soldiers congratulated me on my many aerial victories. *Why, what is this?* I thought. *Have they reconciled with their atrocious past, leaving me to do the same?* I must admit I was shocked by so sudden a turnaround.

Then it struck me. Of course they did not know my faith. Last I was in Austria, I was a forgettable nobody. And a child. Now I had returned a hero. I was being paranoid and overthinking this matter. I must put it to rest. There was no time to partake in the merriments and carousing the land was known for, much less this kind of nonsense, by God! Instead, I was immediately shepherded back onto the Express, where officers and wealthy aristocrats and famed artists came and went, until we arrived in Istanbul. There, with no time to sightsee and pay homage to the many palaces and mosques of great beauty in the distance, I was shepherded into a dingy, dark naval troop transport alongside a few withered-looking infantrymen and some field support pieces, which set out at night to avoid hungry French naval patrols. We were lucky and made good time. Amidst the incessant lapping of the wine-dark waters against our vessel, we made landfall in Haifa.

Apart from the historical scenery, the town did not seem like much to me. It was dusty and dirty, and there was little to do beyond dine and sightsee, as I briefly poked around the newly completed mausoleum of some beauty belonging to a "Báb," the founder of a faith known as the Bábi. I also browsed a small flea market for interesting material and picked up a small and colorful jigsaw puzzle. The food, whilst flavorful, was too exotic for my liking, and after a while made me yearn for the pickings, however slim, of the home country, which I had not enjoyed since my last leave. Fortunately, the people here are fascinating. The first night I was here, I was sent to a military installation to stay the night. I was greeted in what approached a traditional military style by the garrison present, who were used to German discipline since we had dispatched troops to help put down Young Turk and Arab uprisings in the region. Despite the politeness of these troops, however, I wished to get a better understanding of the population around me and ventured outside the base. I was soon after approached by a quintet of dancers, apparently en route to their venue. A troupe of well-mustachioed entertainers, they traded jokes with me and invited me along with them to take in one of their performances, free of charge. The strangeness of their instruments, not at all terrible in sound, was further favorably balanced by their graceful movements and handsome, willowy, elegant physiques, and a good time was had by all. The night was wild, and before long I was filled with almonds and dates, courtesy of these fine gentlemen who hosted me in their hotel room and taught me a few basic steps after their performance. They laughed, I laughed, and for the first time in a while, life seemed acceptable! I had made a few friends, if ones with whom I could barely communicate through their thick accent and scarcely functional command of German. I went to sleep content, curled up with a few of the other men, who appeared awfully affectionate. It was not unpleasant to me, but it was quite unexpected to see this sudden change in culture from the "propriety" of the West. This propriety appeared all the more absent when I woke up only to find my newfound compatriots, and much of my local coinage, had mysteriously vanished. I suppose they had some honor, though, to leave me my German monies! I had gotten used to alienation from my peers, but outright theft from people I was commissioned to respect and protect, not to mention ones I admired in my own right, was a new experience. Nevertheless, as I grit my teeth at this betrayal, I realized there was no chance of catching these scallywags and made my way toward my new base. At least I still have you, Diary!

The attitude of the Ottoman Turks toward us, their Imperial German allies, varies enormously. From the refreshingly curt, able to answer a straight question (if rarely in passable German), to ebullient, energetic, and hospitable, such that I worry they may be eyeing my wallet. They are human, like anyone else. But though they are on the same side as us and thus are easier to talk to than the people of France, citizens of the enemy that they are, Turkey's culture is so . . . different. I'm sure I have not spent enough time in this land and will reserve my judgement until a later date, when I have more experience, but it will take some getting used to. I must also try to be careful, for though I am a visitor, and though I am a wartime ally, I am not above the law. I know myself to be an emissary of Imperial Germany to these people, so I, along with my fellow Germans, must take care to develop a relationship with them that sees to both the Ottomans and my people.

This alliance with Turkey has been expensive. As a sign of respect between our two cultures and to garner influence within their borders, our government gifted them a cruiser, the *SMS Breslau*, to make up for a withheld ship the British were to send them. This should help seal their belligerence against the other nations that bully them so. However, so far, they have made good on their dealings, and though the Russians have opened up a front with them and continuously launch assault after assault at them, our valiant allies have done their best to hold. They have been thrashed at almost every turn but do not seem intent on giving up easily, even as forces of the Americans have begun their march from North Africa through opportunistic, but neutral, British lands and into the outskirts of the Ottoman Empire.

As I am picked up by a staff car, entirely out of place alongside the camels, horses, donkeys, and mules of the streets, I reread my orders. I have been tasked with helping in the training of their small air corps, a motley collection of outdated craft, to fly well enough to rival the mediocre (American) fliers of some of the greatest (French) machines in the world. It will be a challenge, to say the least, but I have, in the past, achieved the impossible before and that gives me hope.

8 February 1918

After a few days of driving in a vehicle proffered to me with my new batman and translator, a paunchy fellow named Ali, I have come upon the airfields of Three Filo, deployed at long last to the Sinai-Arish, specifically, as their rittmeister. Alas, the territory was in a dilapidated state. Stray cats and dogs wandered the fields. These fields, full of rickety, run-down aerocraft dating back to the 1900s, if still armed, were dispersed about the area with reckless abandon. I noticed termite-eaten, but still upright, hangars available. *Why not use them?* I thought as I shoved the sliding doors open. There I found supply crates and a gaggle of men, many still asleep in sleeping bags.

They used the hangar as a barracks.

Further inspecting the area, I noticed we had no fortifications or defenses around the airfield to speak of; even the pilots looked a little threadbare. Our forces are outnumbered and outgunned at least five-to-one in the air, as I had been told by local onlookers on the ride over. Now, I looked them over judiciously before speaking.

"My name is Schaefer!" I greeted them, whilst Ali translated. "I understand we have quite a fight on our hands, but it is my job to whip you all into a trim outfit, able to take on whatever is thrown at us. You may be living like barbarians, but with Germany as your ally, you will learn to fight alongside the best of us. No matter the odds, we will protect your homelands and will enjoy sweet victory or die trying!"

"It is not just that," a scholarly-looking fellow named Mohammad spoke up, introducing himself and shaking my hand as he spoke. "We have heard that some of our . . . subjects amongst the Arabic peoples are being rallied to arms against us, that they, too, may claim lands of their own."

"Does not your Sultan treat your subjects well?" I inquired, curious to know his opinion. The Turkish fliers looked nervously at each other. A damning statement. I began to wonder why our nation sided with them. I changed approaches. "What's to be known about their strength?"

"They are not many, but they move quickly and scout well. Their camels can also travel through difficult terrain with relative ease," replied another fellow, short and hairy, who shrugged when I asked his name. "If they join forces with the Americans, all will be lost, for the leader of the rebellion is a natural strategist."

"Does he have a name?"

"He is a Welshman named Lawrence, and he has been attempting to unite the Arabic people against us for some time, citing that we are tyrants. His goals do not matter, as it is clear that, with backing from Americans, he can be seen as a serious threat. And even if his camel and horse riders do not overrun our airfield whilst we are on the ground and destroy us, the Americans will have our heads with their superior craft!"

"Why, do not talk like that," I exclaimed. "I can show you how to fight, and I'm sure your government will provide better aerocraft for us eventually!"

There was general laughter at that. I began to wonder if I had been sent on a suicide mission in punishment for all the chaos and entropy I had caused the German Empire as a Jew and alleged (and actual) homosexual.

"The Black Jack, General Pershing, commands seventy thousand men," another pilot said. "And we are lucky it is not more. We can thank the combined navies of Turkey and your Germany that the odds are not worse. Our transports have been supplying us with guns and harrying and sinking enemy troop transports at every opportunity they can." He was tall, gaunt, and looked somewhat grim at the moment. "Still, our forty-five thousand under Djemal Pasha look pretty pitiful by comparison." He snorted at the field commander's name. "I am Aslan, by the way." He smiled. "You believe you can teach us to fight well against these odds?"

Verdammt.

"We—well, we shall hold like the Spartans did, I suppose," I said at length, smiling half-heartedly, before wondering if they even knew Greek legends. "Or perhaps, since we are near Troy, I shall be Odysseus, and will do my best to guide my fellow Ithacans and our allies through the war alive!"

Ali looked at me questioningly, but translated.

"I'll try not to suffer the fate of Telamonian Ajax, then, while retaining his strength!" declared Mohammad.

There was a general silence as everyone stared at him.

"Why do you stare? I adore the Iliad!"

9 February 1918

Forgive me, dear Diary, as I wrest you from the jaws of one of the semi-feral dogs who have made the aerodrome their home. It seems they made use of you as a chewing toy, unbeknownst to me, in the hustle and bustle that continues to plague our squadron. Amidst this chaos, all I know is that the American Expeditionary Force has been attempting to push into the area, but our army has thankfully yet to be overrun. Nor will they ever be so. Run-down and overworked though they may be, I find the men to whom I am assigned doing their best, which is all anyone can ask, and with me, they will do better. I hear tell of the Russians pressing the Turks hard from the north, but the Turks have yet to capitulate, and will win, damn them! The nearby Turkish Army is as well entrenched as any position along the Somme with an ingenious network of tunnels to boot, and though we may not quite have other conditions in our favor, I will train Three Filo to dominate the air.

This squadron is composed of a total of eight pilots and six planes. Five of these pilots made it through basic training by Turkish reckoning, whilst three more tagged along and, in the heat of the moment, were taken on board. Turkish high command wanted additional German supervision to grace these fine young men with our wit and wisdom, and who were we to decline? We are allies after all.

And yet, it turns out, after observing them for only a day of flight, that these airmen already have a surprisingly strong grasp of the core concepts of aviation. It appears those who did not have already died, considering the depleted state of the squadron. As we took to the skies, I had them follow me and we gamboled amongst the clouds, executing basic maneuvers, and even Immelmann turns and loops. After watching this progress, I decided to test their gunnery acumen, and was delighted to see that some were even reasonably good shots. Each was able to chase and down the balloons I loosed for them, and one or two of our valiant eight could blow the floating gasbags out of the sky at a remarkable distance. I would have considered it luck, but the consistency of these successful long-range kills was startling.

"Pretty talented fliers are we not, rittmeister?" one of the pilots, Alp, asked of me that evening over kebabs, seeming to have observed a look of shock upon my face. "You know, I knew several of these men from before the war. It is not only you Germans who enjoy the study of flight from the comfort of aviation schools. Four of us hail from various chapters of the Turkish Society of Aviation. There is one in Istanbul, another in Ankara."

It was interesting to know that their origins were not unlike mine! The two of us talked late into the night of our hopes and dreams for aviation and proceeded to clean up after the other pilots when the day had concluded. He was quite a fellow, Alp, and his passion for flight was great as he spoke in the manner of a visionary, describing great aerocraft used for mass transportation, always with great veneration as I was his commander and a veteran aviator—though with such lackluster discipline in the ranks, coupled with loneliness in my life at this time, I'd rather he just see me as a friend. I ended up relating this to him and he laughed, inviting me into town with him the next time he had leave or perhaps to go shopping for food for the squadron. There, he declared, were a population of fellow "people of the book," too, he said. "Perhaps you might find even more friends there!" When I informed him that whilst I had my areas of academic interest, I was no professor nor had much authority on the topic of books, he smiled knowingly. "I meant Jews!"

"How did you know?" I responded. He laughed, tapping his nose. "You all look alike."

I grimaced at that, and he apologized. "I meant no offense!" he replied regretfully, eyes full of concern as he wrung his hands. "It sounds like you have been made fun of before."

I looked at him dead on. "Too many times to count."

"I am sorry. Let me play you a tune to help you forget your troubles. You shall not be bothered again for your faith when you are amongst us."

Alp serenaded me with all manner of curious drums and stringed instruments, his eyes never wavering from my direction, and it was not long before I was enthralled with the exotic tunes and beats to which I could not help but dance a little, much to our mutual amusement. It was a wonderful night and by the end of it we had become thick as thieves, with Alp going on to admit when asked whether or not he had a girl waiting for him that he had never so much as kissed a woman. I responded, remembering Christianne, that I had been kissed, but never kissed one myself. "Unrequited love, rittmeister?" he responded. "You are a most unlucky fellow, sir."

We both burst out laughing at our misfortunes in romance. "At least we have each other!" I replied. Through tears of mirth, Alp could only nod, and we hugged. He had a firm grip and I felt very secure in his embrace. It took much willpower not to tousle his thick, curly black hair.

The only problem I had, which, for now, is entirely beyond my control, is the quality of the craft we had to work with. I recall the first time I took a concentrated look at the field arrayed within the airfield limits. It was an exercise in willpower not to break down in helpless laughter. Three ancient Fokker E.IIIs, within which many of us German pilots *began* our career. A pair of knockoff Airco DeHavilland 2s—pusher designs, good for their day . . . back in 1915. Then the pride of our fleet—a beaten up Nieuport 11 whose time had also long passed. You cannot fly these machines anymore against the modernized contraptions of the enemy! And whilst our current foes are notably focused on our ground forces at this time, I am sure this will not last! If the Yanks see us putting up a fight, they will be sure to contribute additional pilots to the entanglement in the air, which would soon see our demise, allowing them to afterward assault our soldiers on foot with impunity.

We will do our best though.

Watching each aerocraft carefully, I focused my eagle eyes on critiquing their performance as fliers. It was a challenging task. They were eager to please and I did not wish to hurt their feelings, yet it was imperative that they learn to fly as well as possible, as it could be the difference between life and death. Fortunately, I was able to adapt, and my charges were understanding. "Don't forget to reduce speed on your turns!" I would say, miming the slowing of the throttle of the aerocraft. "It will make you more maneuverable. And always try to keep the sun at your back in a fight! The enemy will be unable to track you as easily through the glare."

Though it was a challenge to translate these suggestions through Ali, who was one of the few Turks present who spoke German, it was clear the effort I made at not just ordering improvements, but explaining them, was appreciated.

12 February 1918

Two days of brutal critiquing, grueling advice-giving, and additional training later, many of the fellows were beginning to succeed at the most challenging and rigorous exercises I could think of. If they were not so much ready for a fight before, they now had the fight thrust upon them, in any case. I was confident they would acquit themselves well. As they had learned the arts of aviation from me, I, their teacher, must in turn be taught by my students: I fervently believe that I should begin to put forth a more concentrated effort at learning Turkish. Beyond communicating with my fliers, I must earn the trust of my men, and help them understand that I am putting my best foot forwards in coming to meet them partway and doing my part in what is best for the squadron.

But yes, to the fight. Today we were called upon to scatter to the skies and do our dirty work whilst Turkish ground soldiers were attacked once more along the Sinai Line. As we awaited further intelligence reports, we saw a screen of dust and sand approaching, signaling the advance of foot, horse, and camel. From above us, too, came a pair of Royal Aerocraft Factory R.E.8, distinctive by their engine noises and cumbersome maneuvers. Their roundels marked them out to be American.

The two slow but potentially deadly observer-bomber craft thrummed along dutifully, bereft of an escort in their confidence that they could handle anything thrown at them as they helped undo our valiant hoplites entrenched in the forts of the Sinai Peninsula, the only protection preventing our airbases from being overrun. It was time to take action, whether or not we were prepared.

Now, upon ascertaining this information, I turned to my pilots, deciding which I would take to the air alongside me to intercept this wing. Informal as they were, I decided to allow the pilots at my command the freedom to call one another by their first name, and so, I shall record the two mülazıms (roughly equivalent to our leutnants) I decided to take up with me by *their* first names. Alp and Aslan, they were, one aforementioned as stout and hairy, a pig in a flight suit, whilst the other was tall and gaunt, with a bushy, extremely well-cared for and elegantly waxed mustache. It was they, who, along with Mohammad, possessed some knowledge of German and helped translate to the pilots their mission. These two fellows lack Mohammad's more dignified nature and keep morale up with their never-ending acts of slapstick comedy and wisecracks, which seem to amuse the pilots and therefore bring a smile to my features. "Alp? Aslan?" I inquired, as the two leapt to attention with a comical flourish. "Fancy a dance with the Americans?"

"Something fast and dangerous?" Alp replied, in halting German.

"We'll be happy to cut in, certainly," Aslan, the better-educated of the two, responded with glee. They were dutiful in their conduct, and jumped to action at once, despite being beset by terror at the size and payload of weapons handled by the two-seater enemy craft. We took to the sky, nevertheless, me in the rust bucket that was the British Airco DH.2 pusher from 1915, and the leutnants in a pair of Fokker Eindeckers, fully aware that if we were all to go down, the command structure of the squadron would be shattered.

Still, an example had to be made.

The other pilots raced each other to their craft, despite not one of them being officially assigned to fly that patrol and all knowing that we had more men than planes, eager to be the ones cleared for takeoff. We sallied forth, fighting for each other, despite our relatively recent first meeting, but as we engaged the enemy under the aegis of Sultan, Emperor, Kaiser, and King, we were nonetheless inspired. I admired their enthusiasm and resourcefulness when it came to matters of warfare, and it was interesting to see that the resourceful Turks were putting into battle obsolete aerocraft belonging to the side they were fighting against, such as the Nieuport 11 and, in other squadrons, SPAD S.VIIs, the only identification of their allegiance the black box on a white field painted on their fuselage and wings serving in the place of a roundel.

As we took to the skies and soared ever onwards, our six machines of varying types surely making an absurd display, the American R.E.8 aerocraft saw us coming and, rather than put up a fight, must have been so disgusted by our lack of decorum that they turned tail. Either way, our secret, that Turkish fliers have a presence in the region, was out. I hoped, now, that we might have them pay for their discovery of it. I decided to focus on the ground fight and directed Aslan and Alp to strafe the small force of Arab tribesmen on camels, vigorously signaling them to dive and attack. Next, I pulled back hard on the elevator of my DH2, attempting to climb ever higher after the opposition. This slowed me down greatly, but the enemy remained not much faster than I, since the R.E.8s were large observation and bombing platforms and were laden down with ordnance. As our painfully slow chase continued, they descended slightly, allowing their dive from above to speed their withdrawal.

Surprised at my good fortune, that they would come onto my altitude, I scanned the skies, and concluded that there were no American, French, Italian, Russian, Romanian, Greek, or Trojan fliers out to fall upon me from above. I charged after the enemy, my engine and propeller safely positioned behind my fuselage as I bravely spluttered along at a paltry 150 kilometers per hour—just about its maximum speed, if you can believe it. I almost believed myself back in 1914 on the Eastern Front.

Alas, I was unable to catch up with these enemy aerocraft. Despite their ordnance, they had a head start and a more powerful engine. Disgruntled, I turned around and headed for home, stewing in frustration. Even as we had kept them from dropping their deadly bombs atop our fortifications, we were unable to keep them from reporting the presence of a Turkish air arm in the area and could not even drop one of them from the sky. *It is an unfortunate day*, I thought, coming to realize we were flying these useless planes against superior opposition in almost every way. My mood suddenly changed, however, as I swooped down upon the small force of enemy cavalry, freshly routed by Alp, Aslan, and our own soldiery along our entrenchments. The Airco DH.2 had a slow pace compared to a modern-day aeroplane, but it had an ideal speed for hunting enemy forces on the ground. It was at that speed, and with a clear, propeller-free view of the battlefield, that my Lewis gun sang, cutting down countless cavalrymen, and, alas, their mounts. Perhaps I had overstepped my bounds in the rules of war, attacking a retreating and harmless enemy, but the enemy had left themselves open to such massacre on foot, and did not the enemy bombers intend to cause havoc upon our own men from above as well? It was no real excuse, but I decided to try to satisfy myself with this explanation as best I could, as they would surely return with their numbers reinforced. As such, I continued the assault until I had run out of bullets, at which point I joined my fellow fliers at our aerodrome, feeling extremely regretful but hoping I had protected my allies on foot in some way by launching this counterattack.

Perhaps the DH2, though ancient, can still serve a purpose after all.

13 February 1918

Diary, our chances of survival have improved materially this day.

To start the day off, the squadron received mail, and I have acquired a number of pretty baubles from my parents today. Carefully enclosed in an elegant package was a monographed rubber stamp of an Albatros D.II, a scout plane I have never flown, but had expressed to my father a dear ambition to do so, so nimble, durable, and deadly a plane they were for their time . . . back in 1916. It felt like ages ago, and aeroplane technology has advanced since then, but it was still a thoughtful gift. They inquired in a letter what it was like to fly so close to the promised land, and I had to admit I had not thought about the concept much. In fairness, I had no such luxury to do so, what with all the killing going on. War truly does distract an individual from the true loves of their life. Personally, I'd love to get back into swimming and horticulture, and maybe adopt a dog, but I have been blindsided with work, much of it requiring grim determination from me to not go mad over. To see friends and even foes come and go hurts me, but it seems the best way to overcome this grief is to fight on. I am only a short flight from Jerusalem, and it is only the myriad entanglements with the foeman that keep me from visiting the city of my ancestors, and, I have learned, the third most holy city of my allies. It is in good hands and well-protected by the Ottomans, but a quick discussion with high command betrayed a reluctance of my Turkish friends to allow me leave to explore my roots. They assured me that if the foeman is routed, I shall be the first they will congratulate with this honor. They also warned me about being too free in my expression of my roots—Turkey's wartime government harbors a certain intolerance of other cultures, and whilst they accept many still, diverse an empire as it is, there were anti-war rumblings in Armenia amidst regions of Greece under our control not long ago that were abruptly, some say suspiciously, curtailed, which severely worries me, even as I recognize the necessity of their allegiance to our cause. Nonetheless, it appears a great many Armenians had to be marched to camps away from the front to help them avoid being shot whilst in the line of fire as the Turks clashed with the Russians. I seriously question it was for their own safety, however, as one of the pilots, in fact, our very own resident mythologian, Mister Mohammad, reported that he had not heard from his brother-in-law, a Greek with a penchant for writing letters, for some time now, and that it worried him. It did indeed sound like something to be concerned about, and I promised him that I would attempt to wield what government influence I had to ascertain what happened. It seemed an empty promise, however, as it occurred to me that the only world in which my home government would be willing to risk injuring relations with Turkey the better to help my compatriots would be in one where pigs fly.

This gives cause to wonder. Would pigs fly better than my beaten up DeHavilland craft?

Bearing my earlier thought in mind, I encouraged the men to fight harder than ever to keep their minds off what the government encouraged them to be fighting for, in favor of what they *wanted* to be fighting for. Their sweethearts, their children, their homes, for example. For myself, I pray daily to Hashem that such indignities need not continue to be visited upon the Armenians and never again be visited upon my people. For I fight to ensure my people need never displace themselves again. That we all need never war again.

Though no such matters appeared resolved soon thereafter on that front, a miracle struck the next day in the form of twelve, *twelve* new, enormous crates that were off-loaded from a nearby railroad and wheeled onto the overgrown airfield by donkey-drawn wagon. Straight from Stuttgart, they came. Some of my wilder fantasies were suddenly realized in one fell swoop.

The Fatherland had come through for us once more.

Despite some faltering on the Western Front, what with a new Franco-American offensive, we had scored so many successes along the Russian lines that high command felt confident enough to bestow upon our Turkish allies and, through them, me, some reinforcement craft. Indeed, no longer will we founder about listlessly in obsolete material, but will instead take to the skies in the product of Germany's newest and greatest breakthroughs to date in aviation technology.

Or so we thought.

After some test flights during a suspiciously peaceful lull in the fighting, we, that is, the Turks and I, found that, though handsome and modern in looks, the Pfalz D.IIIa nonetheless did not prove quite as splendid a craft as expected. A product of a different squadron, and thus the wrong place at the right time, I had never flown a Pfalz of any variety, but learned quickly why the German pilot population was not overly fond of them. In a mock dogfight, the D.IIIa outturned anything else in our past arsenal, certainly, and, based on my observation of the enemy and their sizable, but slightly outdated fleet, would put them to shame too. However, they slip as they turn and stall easily in steep dives. They had heavy controls and a low rate of climb, as well. Fortunately, they sport twice as many Spandau machine guns as most craft in the region, can, when called upon to dive, usually do so without shedding their wings, and are very sturdy in a fight. Beggars cannot be choosers, and we hoped to paint the sky red with the blood of our enemies.

They are by no means too good to be true but can be made into killing machines yet. This observation causes me great remorse, however. The fact that I cannot look upon a machine without appraising its ability to kill others almost immediately makes me wonder what kind of monster I have become, though at least despite the murder I had committed, I retain a trace of my humanity, such that I might see my more monstrous side as separate from the rest of me. Still, I am excited to help my allies, the Turks, in protecting what has become their homeland.

Aslan and Alp were overjoyed at the arrival of the packages. Clearly, they had never flown in craft of this quality, as they declared this day one of celebration and treated the messenger and me, whom they called their mentor, to a smoke from their hookah, which they had brought out to celebrate on this occasion; it seems to be their vice of choice, in the absence of alcohol—something the Turks apparently cannot abide. After this tasteful session of vaporized tobacco, which gives such a pleasant burning sensation of the throat, they proceeded to serenade us with oud (a sort of lute) and kemenche (a stringed, bow-driven musical instrument). They then stuffed the two of us to bursting with lahmacun after lahmacun, each a sort of round, thin piece of dough topped with minced meat, vegetables, and herbs. DELICIOUS! I will have to open a parlor that serves this on the menu when I return to Germany.

If I do.

The war is not over yet, and though in this region we have gained a certain sudden advantage for now, the odds may not be with us forever, and a stray bullet is not discerning as to whom it may catch in the head at any time.

5 March 1918

The sky has been awash with targets lately, as my twelve-pilot Filo, now reinforced in people along with our new craft, struggles to duel air forces many times over in size. Meanwhile, the tribesmen led by that vigilante Briton, "Lawrence of Arabia," he is called, continue to work closely with the Americans and French. With horse- and camel-drawn guns, he pounds our army's fortified positions with observation balloon-sighted artillery, the courtesy of his allies, before surging forth with infantry and cavalry, time and time again under support from their bombers, not just American-flown R.E.8s and F.E.2s, but French and Italian-flown Breguet BR.14s and Caudron G.4s. We have managed to repulse their attacks thus far on each occasion without routing, but are slowly being pushed back and are far from safe, with the Turkish soldiers below us reporting significant casualties with each enemy sortie. As we entertain these messengers, I see through their stoic faces their fear and low spirits, betrayed by their stammering voices and eyes red-rimmed from tears, noticing they are close to breaking, and the feeling soon spreads around our base. It fills my heart with dismay to see our men frozen up, or in tears, panicking perhaps rambling on about how we will lose the war. To keep morale up and pass time, I have treated the men kindly and attempted to be respectful of their culture, going so far as to learn the oud, myself, as it seems like a pleasant enough instrument.

Well, when they play it, at least.

I'm still new to the art and the device seems to favor its owner. Alp laughed uproariously as one of our enlisted men, a goat farmer named Abdullah, played a beautiful tune on Alp's instrument before passing it to me, and one of the strings broke almost at once on my touch. It was embarrassing, but fortunately Abdullah was not upset. "These things take time, sir, worry not," he was reported to have said to me with a laugh, according to Ali's generous translation. I felt my face flush with the heat, wondering how much time it would take me to learn the instrument, as well as how much of Ali's translation was contorted out of politeness.

Not to mention how much time I have left before I shuffle off this mortal coil in some way or another.

Morbid thoughts aside, however, for all my efforts, I have become a rather cosmopolitan individual—a Jewish Imperial German pilot from Austria-Hungary who has tasted the culinary wonders of France and Belgium as well, and now revels in the wonders of the Great Ottoman Turkic cultures. If only all the world could see the wonders each nation has in store, perhaps we'd fight less and work together more. Unfortunately, in the middle of wartime, such beliefs are unlikely to be popular. I must keep my mind on fighting, lest I perhaps be forced to reprimand myself for inadvertently spreading seditious sentiment.

Today alone, I have already flown in two sorties. I have gunned down an observation balloon whose findings were allowing artillery to wreak havoc upon friendly lines, as well as patrolled those lines later today in search of enemy bombing craft attempting to breach our positions. In our new Pfalz scouts, I could have easily accomplished both sorties whilst still in the sky, partially due to the larger fuel capacity and more due to the larger ammunition capacity in each craft, but we were encouraged by high command to take a respite between missions, as they wished to conserve pilots and did not want us to take undue risks.

My missions were all the more successful as a result. It appeared the Americans and French were both under similar orders and were loath to decisively commit their air corps in large-scale engagements. This only served to work against them. In addition to facilitating the undoing of the observation balloon, I chased off a pair of "Harry Tates," as the British, and now their American clients, called their wretched R.E.8 craft. The latter were easy targets, as one need only climb at them from below and behind to avoid their rear-facing machine-gun emplacements. As volunteers fighting in France with the Lafayette Escadrille, the official American Expeditionary Forces are reckless, their attacks ill-conceived, and their belief in their inherent superiority as Yankees over their Turkish foes seems to make them think themselves invincible as they trundle through the air en masse. Their army was slowly beginning to better understand stratagems and tactics of this new era, or so it was reported, but their aeroplanes and pilots had a long way to go before being able to challenge our own aviation corps on a one-on-one basis. Unfortunately, considering their numerical superiority, they didn't need to duel us one-on-one.

If Tommy Sopwith had decided to sell anything more terrifying than his Sopwith Aviation Company-designed triplane to the Americans and their French allies on this front, things might have been different. But, because Sopwith Aviation was shipping their best craft to France, and to both sides at that, my men and I decided we were safe to feast upon these Tripes, as well as early-era SPADs and Nieuports sent to intercept our missions, and so, with heavy hearts, we did. Plane after plane fell from the skies, and many good men were needlessly lost.

I was not entirely without mercy, however. I remembered the courtesy my bosom friend, the late Henri DuCoq, once showed me and resolved to be harsh, but fair. Returning the kindness the Frenchman offered me, I would once in a while let the odd outflown pilot escape and offer a jaunty wave as I turned away from the battle. There had to be some humanity, some humility, in war. The ilk of DuCoq is a dying breed, but I was insistent upon carrying on the banner of "white knight" in his name. I must be careful, however, as fliers, regardless of their nationality, are no longer proving as genteel as those I have happened upon in the past, and I am sure both my government and that of Turkey would not be pleased to see me sparing pilots in the spirit of 1915.

As men are struck from the sky, whether by my hand or that of my friends or foes, the survivors, presumably on both sides of the war, grow closer to their remaining allies. Alp, an expert pilot but ever emotional and in need of support from time to time, has sought my counsel on occasion, and the two of us, especially, have grown rather friendly, if Monsieur Diary catches my meaning.

Though it is perhaps a little unprofessional, and indeed, you'd think I'd have learned my lesson from Jan Schultz's conduct, he has recently favored me with a gift, a friendly one with no awkwardness and borne out of a genuine interest I have—an oud of my own—and I am now dead set on mastering the damnable contraption. Interestingly, his father was a builder and repairer of such musical instruments. Alp himself plays drums, oud, and, in an interesting homage to elements of his family's once-Russian side, the accordion! A true virtuoso! Together, we play as Aslan sways and dances to the music, making us kebabs, his talent being that he is the best man to crew the mess in Three Filo. Though this is not saying much in comparison to the other aviators, his own skills surpass any German (and most French) cooks I have encountered. This turned out to be unsurprising, for he later revealed he attended a culinary institute in Istanbul, only to be thrown out later for slighting the traditions of the establishment and being too experimental.

"Here," he declares, slamming some lahmacun on my desk. The flatbread splattered slightly. "A new recipe. I stole some of your chocolate and heated it into an egg, some chilis, tomatoes, onions, and peppers, and a dusting of cheese and meat, and made a manner of sandwich for you, should you wish to roll it up." He chuckles. "It's messy as blazes and travels through the body quickly, but it's delicious." He raises his voice comically to the heavens, shaking his fists in the air. "Laugh at me now, ICI!"

And whilst the Istanbul Culinary Institute maybe didn't laugh at him, we of the squadron laughed with him, and a merry laugh it was too, with delicious results.

The egg was a bit peculiar, but the rest went down just fine and altogether it was a lovely work of art and aesthetically pleasing too.

Despite the dearth of hired hands and pilots for the squadron, things continue to go fairly well. The three of us have bonded like glue, perhaps, in hindsight, at the expense of my fellow fliers, who maybe feel alienated or intimidated even as we allow them to join in on our festivities! Speaking of festivities, it seems as though I have not kindled the lights of Shabbos for some time. Though there is more to Judaism than celebrating holidays, I hope I have not forsaken my family traditions and roots in favor of new and exotic cultural norms and fascinations. I must be like the Jews under Alexander the Great and keep an open mind, amplifying my beliefs through the teachings I have learned from others.

Hmm. I will keep this in mind. A messenger has arrived bearing what appears to be very exciting news. The pilots are in an uproar, so I shall report in a moment.

Dearest Diary, We have received news that Russia has pulled out of this great conflict of arms! By God! This is extremely fortuitous news! It appears the rumblings of their peasants, having developed into an unmistakable roar of the masses, proved too much for the czarist throne, as the people, having successfully taken over, brokered a peace treaty with our Empire!

It is almost too good to be true. With Russia defeated, the war is all but won. Only France and America, as well as Italy, remain as the major powers on the enemy side, though to consider Italy a major power is questionable, as their sizable military, whilst well-equipped, is extremely poorly led. Indeed, their main army is currently being pounded by a surprisingly formidable Austro-Hungarian resistance along the Isonzo River. However tragic their losses, and indeed all nations' losses, the Entente is sure to fall to our superior arms soon, as our veteran guardsmen and hardened regulars can now transfer to the Western Front and bolster their equally weary comrades in arms in France. The Turks, slowly being beaten back in the north, are now also able to focus their armies along the Sinai. Even usually toothless Austria-Hungary has offered up troops in support, having survived their drawn-out war with Russia in one piece! Curious. I would have expected *their* downfall first!

Upon hearing the news, all Turkey, I am sure, sighs in relief, much as the squadron did before it broke out in joyful celebration with a cacophony of shouts and songs, as well as the occasional prayer, of thanksgiving. After making some inquiries, I came to the understanding that, after a very ill-conceived Ottoman assault against Entente lines in the north, attempting desperately to break the enemy in one go, a coalition of Greeks, Serbs, Romanians, and Russians had counterattacked, shattering the main Ottoman positions on the outskirts of Istanbul herself and were snapping at our soldiers' heels as Turkish troops retreated into the city and called for assistance from the local militia and Sultan's own guard. This must have been especially disgraceful, as the Entente advance rolled up in weeks what was an initial Ottoman attack that plunged deep into Greece, but at great cost and took years to make the progress it made. Rumor had it that the Russians had advanced so far, they could hear the call to prayer from the minarets of the Hagia Sophia before they received word of a socialist revolution and the war's end for them.

Upon hearing so, the Russians, who were the main brunt of the Eastern Coalition Army, quickly abandoned the fight, obviously exhausted after their long string of earlier defeats, even as they seemed to be winning now on this front. They broke for home, leaving their allies gravely outnumbered and, after fierce fighting by a reinforced Ottoman line, forced back.

7 September 1918

Diary, though the year continues in earnest, it appears that, just when we thought the front had hunkered down into a stalemate, we ended up winning the day by the strangest of flukes.

For what seemed like eons, we took each day at a time, flying our patrols and going through the endless motions of warfare. Still outnumbered, still entrenched behind crudely built fortifications, steadily collapsing, our soldiers had to wait for the Americans and French to attack us each time with increasing fatalities on both sides, especially now that Italian ground forces had arrived to assist them. We threw back several of their assaults, and our own men had begun to discuss delivering a counterattack whilst they were reordering themselves. I believed we should attack, but Djemal Pasha, leader of the Turkish troops and orchestrator of the disastrous northern push, from which we barely extricated ourselves, had apparently learned a lesson from that recklessness and wished for us to wait, contending that we needed more men, and proposing that we draw upon Palestinian and Northern Egyptian militias as reinforcement before pushing forwards.

These troops were allegedly already detached from their homeland, used as provincials alongside Turkish regulars despite their lack of training in dealing with the local trouble in Armenia. Apparently, there was an uprising of some sort. Reports disclosed to the soldiery are hazy, and were there not men in front of us trying to kill us, I am sure there would be some considerable consternation in the ranks regarding the fates of the citizenry. All we have been told is that some of the Armenian population disapproved of the way the war had been fought and were displaced farther behind our lines, so as not to join those of the enemy's. I shudder at the strict measures that might be undertaken by the absolutist government present here, but I cannot back out now. Though a warrior on the battlefield, I am backboneless in politics and I do not believe German high command is willing to risk her friends when we are so close to victory. I also realize that there is little I can do to ease whatever tensions came to pass in that area, and though I find the time to put pen to paper to request further disclosure about the activities underway in that region and cite my concern, I realize that based upon my skill set, I must fight here and now to make the biggest impact I can.

In brighter news, when I shook myself free of these notions and flew a patrol over enemy lines later that day, my wingmen and I saw that the Franco-American Army had suddenly turned tail to reinforce against a threat from the rear! Searching the skies for enemy fighters and finding two Sopwith triplanes, one of which we downed, we returned home only to receive a dispatch by means of a real fighter plane—a British Royal Aerocraft Factories S.E.5a, to be precise. She was a beauty of a fast, maneuverable, luxury fighter, the likes of which have never been seen in this front!

Stepping out of this craft came a courier from Great Britain, whom we rendered what hospitality we could, providing for him a pipe and comfortable chair, along with a steaming hot skewer of lamb for a meal. The fellow was not to be delayed, however, and begged to report that the Crown Forces of George V had, in fact, gone rogue. In a shocking turnabout from their declaration of neutrality, the armed forces had put serious pressure on their home government and appear to have all but forced them to declare war on the United States! Their casus belli? The United States marched through Cairo without their consent and with intent to invade our lands and theirs as well to achieve a quick victory, having grown tired of watching British arms slip into Turkish ranks. The British-Cairo garrison, composed of some tough Australians as well as their English allies and some local auxiliaries, launched a series of partisan attacks on the Americans, the French, and the token Italian force with them, pinning them down using sneaky tactics that would cost the enemy in blood, but would not last forever.

Say what you like about our . . . middling commander, this was the opening Djemal Pasha needed. After he ordered an attack across all lines, the Turkish Army sallied, and we of the air force did our part, strafing enemy airfields and destroying grounded fighter planes and killing pinned down infantry where they stood, challenging their reign over the sky.

It was not long before the entire enemy force, disorganized and under duress, less superior in their numbers than before and without cover, found themselves in great disorder, falling back to Cairo's port with our men and the English and Australian New Zealand Army Corps nipping at their heels. Not every foeman could escape, however, and before our attack bogged down, we had struck down seven thousand men and captured some fifteen thousand more. Though they still outnumbered us, they were diseased, bloodied, possessed of a battered morale, and isolated: surrounded, save for the Red Sea behind them, at Cairo Port.

An astonishing victory!

With this front temporarily stabilized, I took stock of matters at hand. In the face of the bloody fighting over the course of my tenure at this front, I have lost six pilots and eight aerocraft. Thank God for the four-man squad of reinforcements we received, as the six men we lost constituted half a squadron without them. Truly, the arrival of the Pfalz fighter craft was a mixed blessing, for it made my men cocky and fight with a renewed but arrogant vigor. Nonetheless, my friends Alp and Aslan, alongside much of the rest of Three Filo, continue to survive. Thanks to their personal skill, the quality of our craft—which has enjoyed a brief period of superiority for some of the campaign—and, they insist, my personal leadership, almost every member has scored at least one kill and a handful have scored the requisite five victories that allow them ace status. This is, in part, thanks to the wasteful overconfidence of the United States Army Air Corps, though I will admit that with the assistance of the French and Italians in the region, they were inspired and trained to fight better. Indeed, as the Frogs began to distribute their prized SPAD S.XIIIs, their sneaky pilots, having begun to use Boelcke's tactics against us, committed themselves increasingly well, and I had all the more reason to impose strict orders upon my men, instructing them to flee at the first sign of great numbers of scouts and fighters of our quality, knowing their pilots could, in addition to outnumber us, now very well match ours for training too.

It was an especially dismal loss to see Mohammad struck down. It was during a bombing raid in which he was so quick to scramble his craft, he did not belt himself in, and, in attempting to intercept the bombers, was set upon by the American Ace of Aces, one Eddie Rickenbacker. Out on a lone patrol of his own, this Yank, with a noticeable twenty-three kills since the beginning of the American war, dove from the clouds in a salute to the Dicta Boelcke (the book of tactics written by my acquaintance Oswald Boelcke by which we Germans fought and died), and, in a display of great marksmanship behind the machine guns of his nigh peerless SPAD S.XIII, shot Mohammad's craft full of holes. In swerving to shake this formidable foe, our prized professor of the classics overturned and tumbled from his craft and to his death. He was a good man and a great mind, and to see him fall was a devastating blow to the squadron, who gave him a hero's burial amidst a great many tears and expression of fond memories. He was in the middle of writing a scholarly work of some sort or another on the evolution of Royal Flying Corps aerocraft, religiously studying the wreckage of his foes' aeroplanes on this front and keeping in contact through letters with other technically minded people on other fronts. It appears he will never get a chance to finish his piece.

With the Italo-Franco-American Expedition Force chased back to Cairo and pinned down by British and Commonwealth troops, we of Three Filo find ourselves entitled to an unusual amount of downtime, only occasionally called upon to strafe enemy positions or make a show of strength. In view of our increased amount of time to ourselves, Aslan suggested we take some leave to celebrate our victories so far. The two of us, accompanied by Alp, returned to Haifa, leaving behind Mehmet, a three-kill flier with a passing bit of leadership potential, to run the aerodrome in our absence.

Dusty a town though it remained, it was wonderful to see civilization once more. The populace seemed similarly joyous to see us, in turn, as they bustled out to greet us and put on a small musical display in our honor. With oud and with drums, we responded in kind, and dance competitions ensued until dinner, facilitated in part by Aslan. Delighted by the appearance of dancers, he bumped aside the musicians' conductor and took over for himself, wildly flailing his hands as though possessed by the power of music itself.

As the musical celebrations ended, the true festivities began as dinner arrived, provided by the locals at a nightclub. Improving the scene further in the eyes of many were women who came before us and began to dance in a way that was meant to interest us. As the crowd hooted and hollered approvingly, and the women integrated some of these bystanders into their dance, I found some joy in their skill and grace myself, though I politely turned down their beckoning, taking no interest in their physical beauty, admittedly amplified by their graceful hip shimmies and welcoming belly rolls. This frustrated me and probably them as well. Why could I not be like the others, be normal? Though I quickly reminded myself that there is no normal amongst humans, as we are all so different, and that there were sure to be others like me out there in this sense as well. This restored my flagging morale somewhat.

To remain composed, I distracted myself by seeing to my men, ensuring they behaved themselves and hoping they were not amongst the crowd members who were catcalling these talented dancers. Interestingly, whilst I noticed that though Aslan was starry-eyed by the display, Alp's reaction was not unlike my own—disinterested and distracted. A possibility crossed my mind as I looked my comrade over, wondering, if not hoping, that he might feel for men in an intimate sense. He was not overly handsome, to be sure—I was more for the wiry and thin sort over his porcine appearance—but despite his physique, the hair that covered it was certainly alluring, as was his honest smile, ready laugh, and musical, able mind. When Alp caught my appraising eyes, he smiled back, slightly confused, and waved. Suggesting we look for a place to stay the night. I offered him my hand, and he jovially took it, as we made our way out to the club's front desk where we sought out the proprietor and asked after activities. Seeing the two of us fondly smiling at each other and cracking jokes, as well as holding hands, the gentleman appeared to know of my proclivities and directed us to his "back rooms," or so Alp translated it, on the second floor, where he offered entertainment and safety to those of us of—alternate interests—for a price. There appeared to be little gratitude in this gentleman's mind for the heroics of his nation's aviators. Having seen Aslan off with a few locals to go on a partridge hunt, Alp and I followed the fellow into his den of ill repute.

In this establishment, I found a copy of Rumi's poetry in English and we took turns serenading each other with his works. We then proceeded to play a game of chess, which I found boring, the battlefield tactics reminding me too much of actual warfare, if on an abstract scale. Recognizing Alp felt similarly, we talked instead of our homes and loved ones, when I came to realize that I was, in fact, somewhat bereft of friends and family. When I related this to Alp, he smiled, taking my hands in his own. "You have us now," he said very sweetly. I leaned in to peck his cheek but was rudely interrupted by the den proprietor, who told us that Aslan was waiting for us outside, laden down with dead animals. Time had flown, so we made our way back to our hotel.

Having checked into the room, we noticed that the lodgings were fairly spartan. A set of drawers, two beds, a restroom, and a mirror. Aslan turned to me. "My condolences, friends, but I snore like a thousand hornets. It may behoove us all for me to take this bed for myself."

This forced Alp and myself to share the remaining cot. I shall report, dear Diary, with news of this rendezvous in due time.

8 September 1918

Alp and I remained in the same bed for the rest of the evening, suffering through the racket of Aslan's snoring. That closeness . . . that humanity served to make me feel moderately comfortable. It was no longer early in our business relationship as pilots, and I sincerely doubted he was uncomfortable, and perhaps enjoyed, as I did, the accommodations. Of course, I was not positive of my own romantic feelings toward him, just that I cared deeply for him, but he welcomed my contact when I rolled over in the night, so that was something. Besides, after DuCoq, I was desperate, having been starved for touch, receiving little affection by the Frenchman's hand, merely tantalized, though I did realize he was not to blame.

Alp's furry chest provided great comfort as I braced against it, and as Aslan slept soundly, his roaring snores echoing from his cot, hopefully as comfortable as ours, God bless him, Alp and I cuddled up against each other in the cool desert night.

Rising at a luxurious 9:22 a.m., according to the grimy clock in the bedchamber, we begrudgingly decided that the ravages of war could not wait forever and that we should have breakfast, then return to action. We slowly rose from our bed, roused Aslan, and proceeded to a nearby tavern, where we took our repast.

We were in the middle of a tasty kebab and lahmacun meal when a small squad from the local constabulary made their appearance. They eyed us warily before ordering their meal of the day from the far corner of the establishment. I did not like the look they gave me and was beginning to get a little annoyed by the lack of appreciation the Turkish population was by now showing us, their German allies, and even their own fliers. War weariness I can understand, but we were risking life and limb to protect them!

Alp was less than pleased as well but did not have my willpower. He strode over to one of the law officers and asked if he had any issue with an ally dining amongst fellow Turks. The officer responded in rapid Turkish, but he made it very clear that he did, indeed, feel very unhappy about this development specifically. This was fair, I suppose. Though we were trying to assist in the protection of his empire, I'm sure not everyone was happy about the assistance of nosy and domineering German military advisors and drillmasters in his country, especially as a law officer, and perhaps he had come to learn about my background somehow? Maybe he had been told about the suspicious behavior Alp and I were up to at the club? He could have even been a Young Turk, opposed to German efforts to uphold the Sultan's regime, and as a Jew, I could have upset his vision of a Pan-Islamic Turkey. Whatever the case, Alp's assumption was "right on the money," or so Aslan translated. Aslan then began to pack away the food for later consumption. "Let's go," he said. "We are not wanted here."

As we turned to go, I heard a loud crash and, looking back in Alp's direction, noticed that a scuffle had broken out between my wingman and an official of the law! Not one to escalate a fight on the ground, even in protection of my comrades, I attempted to pull them apart, and got a face full of fist for my efforts. It was a powerful blow and I staggered backwards, my nose bleeding. This gave me cause for outrage, but I tried initially to maintain my temper. I must remember what happened with the DuBois brothers. I breathed in, breathed out. First, the officer insulted me, then, when I tried to break up a fight in my name, but begun against my will, I was struck. Terrible? Yes. Unjust? Absolutely!

But I could overcome that.

Then the rotund officer proceeded to press himself toward me, his grotesque facial expression and rapid Turkish speech flying in my face.

I reflexively lashed back, headbutting the officer.

CRACK!

This laid the man out upon the ground, and though my head ached,

I could not help but feel a sense of victory from my blow. This was not to last!

BIFF!

Just as I laid one man flat, one of his brothers-in-arms had broken away from Alp's attack and laid into me with a terrible blow to the side of the head! I crumpled to the ground, the very foundations of my world spinning about me before I saw black.

10 September 1918

The magistrate heading up the case was respectful, for once appreciating the efforts I put forth in protecting the Ottoman Empire, but did end up ruling that assault of a law officer is a criminal offense, and that the vicious words which began the fight for their part were not. Even as I was struck before I myself lashed out, I was responsible for my squadron men, an extension of my own person. That being said, as a hero of the realm, as well as an allied foreigner, not to mention one who did not provoke or start the fight, he told me he would be lenient toward me, even if I, being Jewish, could not represent myself in court.

Alp, more under the jurisdiction of Ottoman high command, was not so fortunate. Sentenced to forty lashes, so administered by the officer I had struck, who laid into him hard with a sickly grin upon his face, Alp was then promptly demoted and returned to action. The magistrate then sent a telegraph to German high command in the area, the better to deal with me. A considerable hullabaloo ensued as the Germans and Turks argued over terms of my punishment.

It was a complicated situation. The Turks wanted me, a seasoned pilot, to fly on their behalf, but realized that I had lost control and beaten up one of their officials. They did not want this example to go unpunished, that they might not suffer such an indignity again. They also were upset that they could not hold me in their prisons, as the Germans would not hear of one of their own rotting away in an Ottoman prison. Upon being summoned to deliberate, high command back in Berlin wanted to brush the matter under the rug, too, but needed to set an example for the behavior of their own personnel on leave as well and concluded that they all at once wished to uphold the rulings of their Ottoman allies, just not to impound me in their stockades!

And so, I was given a choice. Plead before a German court in Frankfurt or plead before an Ottoman one here in Jerusalem. Thinking of my own safety, even at the expense of my friends, I chose Germany, and will ship off tomorrow. I never even said goodbye to my fellow pilots and I wonder how well Alp will keep order without me.

The remorse behind my decision wracks me. I am unsure if the lads will understand my predicament and hope they will forgive me for my sudden departure or activity, but I know that the war speeds toward its conclusion. The lads have learned well from me and it's time the baby birds fly from their nest. I wish I could join them, but I must be allowed to plead my own case and answer to the crimes I committed, yes, but on my terms.

10 November 1918

Germany, I return to you, but Mein Gott, what disrepair do I find you in.

Of course, you could say the same of me. I am bereft of my comrades, whom I may have consigned to death, and am delivered from an Ottoman prison by merit of my laurels alone. It is dismal indeed to consider that I have avoided damnation, fairly and squarely placed upon me for attacking someone on the ground, and by visiting cruelties upon others in the air—fifty-one others, at that! I did not wish to speak much about the incident but was called to the box to defend myself against the crime of assault upon a constable. Advised to plead not guilty and told to explain that I was only pulling apart the two pugilists, I, in a state of great melancholia, instead pled guilty and prepared myself to be hanged by the neck. I would never win the great respect I desired for both myself and my people and wanted nothing more of this war, especially with so sullied a reputation as I already had, now made worse. Unfortunately, the judge was lenient.

"Schaefer," said he, glowering down from the judge's box, adjusting his big white wig, "you've done wrong, but haven't we all? If you can promise us you recant your wild and raucous ways, we will, by merit of your fifty-one enemy kills and rank of oberleutnant and squadron rittmeister, rescind our charges. You could return to the front!"

Ruefully, I shook my head. "I am finished with killing," I said. "I want nothing more than to go home and live out a house arrest. You wish to admonish me? I am amenable to these terms."

"Then you shall not have them," the judicator replied, scoffing and pounding his gavel. "This is a punishment, not an arrangement. You will be redeployed at once to the Western Front, restrained from ever returning to the Ottoman Empire. At the front, you will be called upon to train, but not to fight alongside, our allied British pilots. We no longer have stock in the Palestine front, as the Ottomans are confident they can finish the fight themselves, and we must finish our fight in France. Train the Tommies until the war's end and you will be absolved of your crimes."

I nodded reluctantly before striding off.

"Oh, and Schaefer?"

I turned around.

"Touch one hair on the head of *our* military policemen, and you will be imprisoned, not to mention flayed, within an inch of your life."

"Jawohl."

I turned to leave under guard, when, upon leaving the courthouse, to add insult to injury, who should cautiously walk up to me but Christianne herself. Wringing her hands worryingly, she inquired, stammering, if it was indeed truly me, before begging me to stay with her a time and tell her where I had been all these years, inquiring where I was and where I was going.

"Oh, Christianne," I replied, as the guards forced her away from me, "it is wonderful to see you, but I am not, and may never have been, the man you took me to be. I wish you great love and joy in your future. You will do well. I must do what I must do and shall not besmirch your honor."

She grew angry at this, perhaps hurt by my ignoring her all this time, and, through tears, began to hurl slights in my direction. Tears welled up in my own eyes, and I nevertheless tried to appear strong and marched off with my escort.

4 October 1919

Diary, the war has concluded.

After many years of long, harrowing combat, our forces on the Western European front managed to at last coordinate a daring attack that carried the day, month, and last five or so years.

After so many years of endless bloodshed, with the Franco-American and slightly Italian expeditionary force having long been defeated in the Middle East, the Russians having surrendered on the Eastern Front, and the Anglo-German Navy ruling the waves, scouring the sea of French line vessels and American support and supply craft to their allies, we were in a position to at last march on Paris. After nearly a year's worth of planning, a daring amphibious assault was authorized, and under the cover of naval bombardments from our fleets, a Western French front was opened up near the Pyrenees mountain range so as to throw the enemy off. As the transport ships were screened by the destroyers and battleships of the Royal Navy, the Tommies and their colonial allies were mostly unopposed in their initial landing and were able to make great progress in a war of maneuver akin to 1914 all over again.

To cover their advance, our own infantry, and by extension our pilots, were under orders to attack across all sectors, pinning the enemy down so the enemy could not halt the British advance. Losses on all sides were egregious, but the job was done, as the French, seeing that the writing was on the wall, surrendered their arms in the Treaty of Berlin, stipulating that the French cede their African and Asian colonies to Germany as well as another great swath of land from the mainland. Italy was to concede the Dodecanese Islands and Libya, recently won from the Turks, back to the Ottomans along with a sizable indemnity, and Russia was to lose some of their western territories to both us Germans and Austria-Hungary. America would pay considerable reparations to each of the nations on our side, whilst Serbia would lose a portion of its territory to Bulgaria, who had aided in Serbia's annexation alongside Austria-Hungary.

For myself? My duties to give back to society after my crime are completed at long last. It was not a challenging task to train the Britons. Whilst the mostly idealistic ivory-tower university students of the Franco-American Lafayette Escadrille, whom I mentioned earlier, were looking for a little extracurricular activism and a thrill between their studies, many of these newly arrived British fellows, our allies, were hardened mechanics and tinkerers, hands-on with machines and knowing what they were up against in flying a crate.

Because British models were, of our own admission, nearly equal to our own by the end of the war, they were supplied by their own side. Sopwith Camels and S.E.5a scouts mostly, though there was one bomber squadron that brought over some enormous Handley Pages, which compared favorably with even our Gothas in their monstrous size and weapon payload!

All these craft seemed to suit the hands-on individuals well, and they quickly acclimated to the rigors of aviation. Before long, the Jasta Riedesel, a squadron of these Tommies who flew for us, named after Friedrich Adolf Riedesel, a famous Brunswicker soldier who, like Knyphausen, had helped the Crown in the American War of Independence, were ready for action and deployed to the front. After expressing their gratitude by providing me with a beautiful bronze plaque, I heard little more about them as individuals, save that they acquitted themselves as a group rather well. All I know for sure is that I was quick to overhaul the threadbare British training protocols, putting my German techniques to the test, which whipped the groaning, grumbling British pilots into a physical shape they thanked me for. Beyond that, we organized war-gaming nights to improve their tactical and strategic tendencies, had mock dogfights, and trained to survive difficult land conditions too. It was a lark to see, and good for their improved survival and mental acuity as well. For a time, I almost enjoyed it.

I carried out my sentence dutifully, taking great care not to reveal my presence to my family back in Prussia, who would be both confused and scandalized by my assaulting of a constable of the law, ever under the impression that I was very much in favor of working with the goyim. Indeed, in my shame, the easiest way out of this conundrum I could think of was to pay a young man to venture back to Prussia and inform them I had died in combat at the hands of a French flier. This I did, if with tears of regret and remorse in my eyes just the same, for I had meant to show my family we could prosper here, and yet had, myself, failed.

By the conflict's end, I remained one of the deadliest warriors in the sky, known in infamy by my foes and largely swept under the rug by my allies. For indeed, as much service as I had rendered the Empire, the people grew to look upon my alleged death with relative indifference. Whilst I do not really mind, I do find the irony of this tragic. I, a high-ranking ace! I lived for them, killed for them, learned from and enjoyed the company of all manner of other nations, whilst yearning for my own adopted one, and the world still saw me as that Austro-Hungarian Yid with no sense of authority. How their opinions do differ at the slightest change of fortune. They did not comprehend my plight, yet even as they were so caught up in their own lives and lies, they still insisted upon judging me when matters were problematic or ignoring me when they were acceptable. It was a travesty of justice that we could not live and let live, as we German pilots all attempted to do at first alongside the French aviators of the early air war. A curse upon those who would have us duel each other like soldiers!

All these deaths due to nationalist nonsense. There must have been a better way.

How many had lost their lives over a war they were swept into out of love for their nation, to a fault most likely, when each nation itself was swept in by honor?

PAH!

If only this had been a war restricted to the Balkans! But it is too late for that. Damn the laws, I have to see how Alp and Aslan, my beloved friends, have done for themselves.

18 December 1919

The spirit of Turkey's glorious victory over the Entente forces in the Middle East and beyond continued to burn brightly as I covertly stepped off the boat in Haifa once more, this time under the pseudonym Heinrich Schmidt. Ottoman Turkey was somewhat as I had left it, though with a renewed spirit and revivified economy. She had been paid a vast indemnity to satisfy her wartime expenses. Children played football in the streets as elders smoked from their hookahs on balconies above, whilst merchants peddled their wares. It was good to be a Turk this year, and people were reveling in their national pride. Unfortunately, this meant that people were unwilling to discuss the darker side of the war.

Asking a police constable to take me to their magistrate, I was conducted to the same gentleman who had jailed me long ago. Closing the door, so that the constable who did not recognize me would not hear, he shook my hand, remembering my fleecy hair ("Like a lamb," he said!) and furrowed brow when I spoke. Unfortunately, his words were grim when I inquired as to the whereabouts of Alp and Aslan.

"In the final days of conflict, an American bombing raid blew up the magazine to the aerodrome. Your friends were caught in the blast. I am sorry to say this and hurt you. They were recognized as amongst our better pilots and buried with full military honors, at least," he replied mournfully.

Chalk up a point for the Americans, I thought bitterly. Again, fortune has struck me another painful blow. Life has become exhausting with these endless tragedies rained upon me.

"Very well," I concluded, turning to him and glowering so as to make his mustache quiver. "Take me to their graves. I should like to pay my last respects."

The magistrate conducted me to an officer, and the two of us piled into a constabulary lorry. We then drove deep into the desert. Several hours later, having come across little more than scarce brush and the occasional scurrying animal, punctuated by a single oasis, we came across the remnants of the aerodrome. It had been razed, utterly bombed out, but next to it stood a number of headstones, each facing Mecca, with a crescent moon adorning them. I fell to my knees, tears welling in my eyes. I could read their names and easily recall their faces smiling at me: Alp, Aslan, Mohammad. At peace at last with their comrades.

As I stared off into the distance, a hand lightly tapped my shoulder.

"Sir, night is falling. There is nothing either of us can do anymore. Let us return home?"

Still crying, tears stinging my eyes, I allowed myself to be raised to my feet.

I will escape this twisted world of violence, full of traumatizing memories of death and destruction.

I will leave this Godforsaken land, and live as a hermit in the worlds beyond, where aeroplanes are civilian.

And so, I shall make my final sortie—to Costa Rica.

Perhaps there might I soar once more in peace and prosperity.

Joined by the spirits of DuCoq and Alp.

Special thanks to:

Shannon Scott
Beth Wright
Nathan Carroll
Gilah Benson-Tilsen
Veronica Hatala
Jason Grossman
Adrienne Pond